Eunice Gottlieb and the Unwhitewashed Truth about Life

ESPECIALLY FOR GIRLS Presents

Eunice Gottlieb and the Unwhitewashed Truth about Life

TRICIA SPRINGSTUBB

DELACORTE PRESS/NEW YORK

For Paul, again

This book is a presentation of **Especially for Girls**™,
Weekly Reader Books. Weekly Reader Books offers
book clubs for children from preschool through high school.
For further information write to: **Weekly Reader Books**,
4343 Equity Drive, Columbus, Ohio 43228.

Edited for Weekly Reader Books and published by
arrangement with Delacorte Press.
Especially for Girls and Weekly Reader are trademarks of
Field Publications.
Printed in the United States of America.

Published by Delacorte Press
1 Dag Hammarskjold Plaza
New York, New York 10017

Manufactured in the United States of America
First printing
Library of Congress Cataloging in Publication Data

Springstubb, Tricia.
  Eunice Gottlieb and the unwhitewashed truth about life.

  Summary: The summer eighth-grader Eunice goes into the dessert-catering business
with her best friend, Joy, brings revelations to her about change and friendship and new
beginnings.
  [1. Friendship—Fiction.   2. Moneymaking projects]
I. Title.
PZ7.S76847Eu   1987   [Fic]   86-24359
ISBN 0-385-29552-9

Why do we call our generous idea illusions and the mean ones truths?

One

EUNICE GOTTLIEB SAT on the edge of the bathtub, reading "Dear Phoebe."

DEAR PHOEBE:
  Though I have read your column for years, this is my first time writing to you. I never expected to feel so alone in the world that you would be the only person I could turn to. Yet that's the way things have turned out. I desperately need your advice.

  "Eunice, are you all right, honey?"
  Eunice jumped at her mother's voice, calling through the locked bathroom door. The bathroom was where Eunice was forced to read "Dear Phoebe" since her mother definitely did not approve of a twelve-year-old's perusing such stuff. Mrs. Gottlieb had a large stock of Neanderthal notions.
  "I'm fine, Mom," Eunice said loudly, and added, in a hiss, "Now scram!"
  "You've been in there so long. . . ."
  "What'd you do, set a timer?"
  "What? I can't hear you."
  "I said I'll be out in a minute!"
  "You don't need to raise your voice like that!"
  At times like this Eunice fantasized:

  a. Screaming
  b. Having her best friend, Joy McKenzie, conceal her in her bedroom closet till they both were eighteen and could buy a houseboat in which they'd sail around the world

1

c. Writing to "Dear Phoebe" for legal advice on how to disown your family

d. All of the above

In the meantime, she turned back to her newspaper.

"The problem," the letter went on, "is my best friend."

There, thought Eunice, was a contradiction in terms. How could your best friend be a problem? Obviously this poor writer wasn't gifted with a friend like Joy McKenzie. Here was one of the fringe benefits of reading "Dear Phoebe:" Not only did you learn about the Real, Unwhitewashed World most adults were so anxious to keep from you, but you also realized how lucky you were compared with many other people.

"Eunice?"

"What'd she do, fall in?"

"If that's your idea of humor, Millie Gottlieb, you need a head transplant!" yelled Eunice to her big sister.

"Come on out. I have to curl my eyelashes."

"To match your curled-up brain?"

"Eunice?" called Mrs. Gottlieb. "I'm going to stew you up some nice prunes."

The doorbell rang, and Eunice could hear Millie shoot down the hall to the front door. She was expecting her balloon head boyfriend, Richard, as usual. Eunice read on:

"I have known this friend nearly all my life, and until recently I trusted her the way I'd trust my own mother. Phoebe, imagine my shock to discover—"

"Eunice! Open up instantaneously!"

The pounding on the door would have splintered it if Eunice hadn't immediately thrown it open.

"Joy! What's wrong? What happened?"

Joy stood there with bright pink cheeks, her butterscotch-colored hair as wild as if she'd ridden in on a tornado. She was waving the evening newspaper, the very one Eunice had been trying to read, over her head.

"I've got it!" she crowed, pushing the paper toward Eunice. "Here's our summer, right here!"

Eunice took the paper from her. Joy jabbed a finger at a photo of a very large, very happy woman beaming from behind a mammoth tiered cake.

"I was reading the review of Primavera's recital when my eyes just happened to stray across the page. Obviously it was destiny." Joy executed three perfect pirouettes, which made Eunice seasick just to watch. She picked up her own copy of the paper.

"I was just reading the paper too. You won't believe this letter in 'Dear Phoebe'—"

"Egad! How many times have I told you not to diminish your brain on that dribble!" Joy didn't believe in "Dear Phoebe." Her motto in life was: "This above all: to thine own self be true. . . . ." Somehow when Joy said it, it didn't sound like a cliché at all. Other people might sound like walking fortune cookies, but not Joy. She knew her own mind. She couldn't comprehend people asking for advice. Joy was an only child, and if she'd wanted to read "Dear Phoebe," she wouldn't have needed to go sneaking around among her older sister's 2,000 shampoo bottles and her younger brother's moldy rubber ducky. Joy's parents had serene faith in her judgment, and she could have read *The Joy of Sex* with her feet up on the living room coffee table if she'd wanted.

But other people's concerns—except, of course, for Eunice's—held no interest for Joy. She scanned the paper for dance reviews, and that was all. Joy was a dancer, destined for world renown. Eunice believed that fact the same way she had once believed in Santa Claus: if that wasn't true, there was no such thing as truth. Joy was an arrow speeding toward a definite, if still distant, mark.

Eunice, by comparison, was a blob of Play-Doh, and she knew it. For years her mother had introduced her as "Eunice Enid, my sweet, stable middle child." No more. Something had come over Eunice. Or, closer to the truth, something was erupting inside her. For the past year or so she'd felt as if she'd swallowed a geyser, and it wasn't Old Faithful, either, because she could never predict when it would suddenly shoot out. Sometimes she'd find herself in tears for no reason she could name. Other times it was laughter she couldn't stop, or fury that scared even her. And then there were remarks like the one that had come shooting out last week at her school Career Night.

"And what career are you planning, Eunice?" the principal had asked her. He was wearing his concerned, friend-to-all-students smile.

Mrs. Gottlieb, standing there in her good royal blue dress, had looked at Eunice nervously. And Eunice had replied, "I'm going to be a flea counter for the ASPCA."

Out in the hallway Mrs. Gottlieb had grabbed her elbow. "What did you say that for? What's gotten into you lately?"

Eunice wished she could say. All she knew was the fizzy feelings and black moods that came over her had something to do with Real Life. That was why she had to read "Dear Phoebe" every night, to find out as much about it as she could. Sitting on the edge of the bathtub she'd feel alternately terrified and overjoyed at how much she had ahead of her.

Meanwhile, Joy was snatching Phoebe's advice from her hands and hurling it down on the bath mat.

"Dribble! Now where was I? Oh, yes. You know, of course, that I, unlike some people I know, make it a point never to clutter my mind with trivia, but for some reason I started reading this." She pointed to the happy woman and her cake, "After two seconds *voilá!* I saw it all! You and I are in business, Eu!"

"Business?"

"How's this for a name? Have Your Cake. As in 'and eat it, too'— but we'll leave that off; it'll be much classier. Well? What do you think?"

"I think I'd like you to tell me what you're talking about. And don't give me that how-did-I-ever-get-the-world's-densest-person-for-a-best-friend-look, please."

"All right, all right." Joy drew a deep breath and tossed her long amber-colored hair. "You and I are going to run a dessert-catering business. We'll specialize in cheesecake, mousse, stuff like that. My mother has a whole cake-decorating kit she's never used. Too bad I didn't think of this earlier! Egad! We've missed the graduation cake trade. But there are still all the wedding and baby showers, first communions, and Fourth of July bashes, not to mention all the parties people throw in summer just for no reason. It's supposed to be a hotter than normal summer. Who's going to want to be sweating and slaving in the kitchen when he or she can just pick up the phone and order a scrumptious, superrich—"

4

Eunice filled a glass of water at the bathroom sink and held it up. "Joy, stop."

"Professionally decorated and, our major selling point, *cheap*—"

"Stop or I swear I'll dump this water over your head!"

"Strudel, cheesecake, or mousse." Joy grabbed the water from Eunice and drank it down. "Eu, this resistance of yours to new ideas—you've got to overcome it. It's very boring, not to mention dumb!"

"Tell me one thing: Who's going to be making these scrumptious, professional, superrich cheesecakes and mousses?"

"We are! Who else? At least until we become really successful. Then maybe we'll hire some underlings."

"Joy, we don't know how to make that stuff."

"We know how to read, don't we? All we need are some good cookbooks. If Mildred Butts can do it, we certainly can." She pointed a finger at the jolly woman in the newspaper photo. "She started in her own kitchen with her mother-in-law's recipe for strudel. Now she's incorporated. And she worked *alone*, Eu. Think what you and I *together* can do!"

Just then Eunice's big sister, Millie, came in. "I wonder if it'd be too much to ask you two to have your conversation somewhere besides the bathroom?"

"This isn't a conversation," said Eunice. "It's a business meeting."

"Whatever it is, please move." Millie was carrying a lethal-looking instrument which she now proceeded to use to mutilate her eyelashes. Mrs. Gottlieb thought sixteen was still too young for makeup, so Millie had to resort to things like curling her lashes, pinching her cheeks, and biting her lips to make herself adorable. Once, when Millie was driving her particularly berserk, Eunice had considered writing to "Dear Phoebe" about her. "My big sister," she would describe Millie, "who is sadly into self-torture . . ."

"Not only is she incorporated," went on Joy, who never let Millie or, for that matter, anyone distract her, "but she's also putting her son through college. I'm not talking about a lemonade stand, Eu. This is Big Time." She lowered her voice. "You'll be able to buy a lifetime supply of deodorant."

This was a sensitive point with Eunice, who had begun to suspect she didn't always smell as daisy fresh as the deodorant ads

5

said she was supposed to. It wasn't just moods that came over her suddenly and unpredictably these days. Her body, too, had become untrustworthy.

Yet when Eunice asked her mother to buy her some deodorant, Mrs. Gottlieb only smiled. "What for? You smell exactly the way a twelve-year-old girl is supposed to smell. There's time enough for all of that."

"More antiperspirant than you could possibly use," said Joy.

"That would be nice," said Millie. "Then she wouldn't always be sneaking my Ban." She transferred the curler to her other eye.

"I don't always sneak yours," said Eunice. "Only on important occasions."

"Anyway," continued Joy, "the point is this business could give us financial independence."

"But you already have that," said Eunice. "Your parents will give you whatever you want."

Joy drew herself up. Being reminded that she was a potential spoiled brat was *her* sensitive point.

"I said independence. There's something I don't want them to buy me. I want to buy it myself."

Even Millie stopped to stare at that.

"I've decided it's time for me to start private lessons. Every truly serious dancer takes them. Well, you know how my parents feel about my dancing. They keep hoping it's something I'll outgrow, so I can become a brain surgeon or ambassador to the UN. Private lessons are expensive. If my parents scrimped and saved for something they didn't really approve of—I don't want to feel creepy about taking these lessons."

Eunice felt that old rush of love for her best friend. How could you resist someone so pure and dedicated that she looked for ways to make life harder on herself?

"We'll do it," Eunice said. "Let's go to the library this minute and get out every fancy cookbook they have!"

"I have a better idea. Let's go to the kitchen this minute and do those supper dishes." Now Mrs. Gottlieb appeared in the doorway, with Eunice's little brother, Russell, grimy from head to foot, in tow. This was typical Gottlieb: all crowded together in the bathroom, the one place in the house a person might expect to get a little privacy. It was amazing no one hollered down to Mr. Gottlieb in his basement workshop to come up and join the party.

"I'll do the dishes when I get back, Mom. The library's not open much longer, and this is *très* important."

"Eunice, I've had a very long day. Mr. Vanderpool was on the warpath again. The library will be open for two more hours."

"But Mom! The dishes will be there when I get back!"

Didn't she know by now that logic was futile?

"Don't argue, and don't grind your teeth. And before you do anything, you eat that dish of prunes on the stove. Millie, you look stunning. Now *vamoose*, Russell needs his bath."

"Just once," fumed Eunice, "just once I'd like to be treated with a little respect around here!"

"Hey, look at this!" Russell had picked up the newspaper from the floor and was gaping at it, getting even more saucer-eyed than usual. "Look at this gorilla! It has a pet cat!"

"Just once," Eunice went on, "just once in my life I'd like to be treated like an individual human being with rights, instead of a spoke in a wheel. Just once—"

"Look, Eu-eu!" Russell shoved the paper in her face. "A gorilla with a pet kitty."

"Aaaah!" cooed Millie, at the same time wincing as she pinched her cheek. "How sweet! How cunning!"

"How weird," said Joy.

"Weird?" Russell looked stricken. It was a look he got on his face often, every time someone hinted to him the world might not be as rosy as his eight-year-old brain believed. He ran a hand through his hair, which had grass stuck all through it. "What's so weird about it?"

"It's only because he's in captivity," said Joy. "In the wild that gorilla would probably swallow that kitten for a bedtime snack. But since he's caged up all alone, it's the kitten or nothing for a friend."

"Now hear this. I'm not saying it again." Mrs. Gottlieb made a megaphone with her hands. "Everyone, out of this bathroom *now!* N-O-W!"

"Mind if I wash up?" Mr. Gottlieb came in with paint-speckled hands. "The Indians lost again. A five-run lead going into the ninth, and they lost,"

"Ernie, I don't know how you can go on rooting for that team."

"I'm always for the underdog. I can't help it."

"The Indians aren't underdogs. They are dyed-in-the-wool, not-a-prayer-in-the-world losers."

"I still don't think it's weird," said Russell, hugging the newspaper protectively with his round, sunburned arms. "We're ascended from monkeys, you know. So why shouldn't they love things just the way we do?"

"All I'm saying, Russ-o," said Joy gently, laying a hand on his shoulder, "all I'm saying is it's not natural. Gorillas do not naturally go for something so different from them as kittens."

"Yeah," said Eunice. "But if Millie can love Richard, why shouldn't an ape—"

She'd blown it. If only she'd managed to keep her mouth closed, she might have slipped out unnoticed. But now her mother took her by the collar and marched her to the kitchen sink.

"Do you believe I belong to this family?" Eunice grabbed up a dish towel as Joy began to wash. "If my mother and I both didn't have the same funny left big toes, I'd swear . . ."

It wasn't till later, when they were at the library, poring over recipes for Chocolate Vienna Torte and Raspberry Bombe, that Eunice remembered she hadn't finished reading "Dear Phoebe." By the time she got home the paper had disappeared. Her father must have found it and tied it up in one of his neat bundles down the basement. Now Eunice would never know what awful problem that poor writer had been having with her "best friend."

Two

DEAR PHOEBE:

Please help me with this problem. I am pretty attractive except for one thing. My problem is my nose. It is huge. It reminds me of a baking potato.

Ever since I was twelve, I've dreamed of having cosmetic surgery. My mother wouldn't let me. Then later in my life I couldn't afford it.

Now my two children are grown (yes, I somehow managed to marry in spite of having a nose like a bratwurst) and I have saved some money. Do you think I'm silly to want to have plastic surgery at my age? Phoebe, my nose is on my mind morning, noon, and night.

POTATO NOSE

Eunice, sitting on the edge of the tub, read that Dear Phoebe didn't think Potato Nose was silly at all. Looks, after all, were important, and anyone who was thinking about her nose every waking minute owed it to herself to do something about it.

Eunice laid down the paper and stood up to look in the mirror. There was nothing wrong with her nose. It was a very ordinary nose, to match her very ordinary eyes, mouth, and hair. She did have a weird big left toe, of course, but toes were a lot less prominent than noses—especially noses the size of baking potatoes. There was no putting a shoe over a nose.

Yes, reading good old Phoebe should once again have made her count her blessings in comparison with other people. But looking in the mirror, Eunice couldn't help feeling dissatisfied. Here it came—not the geyser, but the thundercloud. Huge and black, it could suddenly, unpredictably settle over her and make her feel so miserable she could barely speak. Now, as she looked in the mirror, the cloud seemed to fill the bathroom, and she silently called: *Breasts, where are you?*

She knew they were there because she could feel a new, gentle soreness when she touched herself. And she knew they were there because shirts that still fitted everywhere else had grown tight across there. But what good did *her* knowing do? No one else could tell. Her entire body had grown rounder and softer, and her breasts just blended in. She had plumped up all over, causing her father to call her his "pierogi," causing Eunice to cry, causing her mother to try to hug her and to yell, "Ernie, for heaven's sake!" at the same time.

"You could do exercises," Joy had advised, "or you could just give your poor body a break. It'll sort itself out in its own good time."

Joy was the only person on earth Eunice could confide her worry in. Joy, the dancer, didn't care about what her body *looked* like, only what it could *do*. Her body was an instrument of art. Now just the thought of her shot a streak of sun through the heavy black cloud. Eunice unlocked the bathroom door and went up to her bedroom, where she took the scrapbook with the red and white covers from its hiding place under the mattress.

She had kept this scrapbook for six years. On the very first page was a photo Mrs. Gottlieb had taken of Eunice and Joy with their arms thrown around each other's shoulders. They were six years old, both grinning and both missing front teeth. "The jack-o'-lantern picture" Eunice called it.

On another page were a pressed wildflower from Brownie camp and a newspaper clipping with a photo of Joy in her first recital; Eunice had been there, of course, just as she had for every performance Joy had ever given. There was also the forged excuse note Joy had written for Eunice in second grade: "Please excuse Eunice from being absent yesterday, because she had the fuel."

There was a scrap of red and white print material, all that was left of a shirt they'd bought together and taken turns wearing till it disintegrated.

Eunice paused at another photo Mrs. Gottlieb had taken of them, on the first day of junior high. Now that she'd survived an entire year at the new school, it was funny to look at herself in the picture, clutching her stomach and grimacing as if about to have half her teeth pulled. Didn't being able to remember how petrified she'd been that morning mean she was still the same person? Yet she wasn't. Since nearly every important memory of her life was connected in some way or other with Joy, Eunice couldn't think about who she'd been or who she was or whether the two were the same or different (here her head always started to spin a little) without thinking of Joy.

Now she paged through the scrapbook until she felt better, then slipped it back between her mattress and bedsprings.

The next afternoon Joy handed her what Eunice knew would have to be the newest entry in the scrapbook: the logo she'd designed for Have Your Cake. Joy's parents hadn't been sending her to art lessons since she was three years old for nothing. The business's name was written in very elegant calligraphy, with both the *A*'s made to look like miniature tiered cakes. Joy hadn't wasted any time: she'd designed the logo, made up little flyers advertising the business, and instructed her father to run off copies at his office, all within forty-eight hours.

HAVE YOUR CAKE

Tired of slaving over a hot stove??? Tired of paying high prices for desserts that aren't always "up to snuff"???

Then just call 555-5824 and leave the rest to us. We are experienced caterers who specialize in such International Delicacies as Sacher Torte, Chocolate Mousse, and Grandma Gottlieb's Famous Apple Strudel.

Our prices are extremely reasonable, *and* we deliver!

So whether it's for a family supper you want to make really special or that very important occasion, call HAVE YOUR CAKE—today!!!

SATISFACTION GUARANTEED

"Experienced caterers?"

"Well. There was that time we made the appetizers for your mother's party."

"Cheez Whiz on crackers! And for your information, my Grandma Gottlieb was only famous for the gingerbread that broke my father's tooth off."

"Who said I meant your Grandma Gottlieb? I'm sure somewhere in the world there's a Grandma Gottlieb who makes great strudel. Besides, this is the business world! Competition is cutthroat! Let the buyer beware!"

They rode their bikes to Fairmount Boulevard, where the fanciest homes in the city were, and stuck the flyers in mailboxes. Then they rode out to the office of the local newspaper and placed an ad. Joy decided on the kind that was set off in a little box, even though this cost considerably more. Eunice sighed as she counted out the last of her pitifully meager allowance. Joy said, "Nothing worthwhile is ever accomplished without risk, you know. Now come on. We have work to do."

While Mrs. McKenzie was at work, they turned the McKenzie kitchen into a laboratory. Wearing scrupulously clean aprons, their hair in nets, the library cookbooks propped up all around them, they performed their experiments.

"Butter."

"Butter."

"Sugar."

"Sugar."

"Six and one-half squares semisweet chocolate."

"Six and one-half squares semisweet chocolate."

"Eight egg yolks."

There was a pause.

"Eight egg yolks," repeated Joy.

"We bought the wrong kind of eggs. These have the yolks and whites all together."

"Of course they do. We have to separate them."

"Are you crazy?"

"Here, I saw my mother do it once," Joy said. "It's all in the wrist."

Ten minutes later Joy stood staring at the mess she'd made. "I guess we could have scrambled eggs for lunch," she said.

"These dumb recipes!" cried Eunice, who couldn't bear to see Joy wilt. "They're so bossy! 'Beat this and add that! Whip to stiff peaks and cream thoroughly!' Who do they think they are?"

Joy smiled. "Maybe we bit off more than we can chew here. Pardon the pun."

Eunice all but pawed the ground. "Ha! Us? If anybody can do this, it's you and me!"

Joy's smile widened. She socked Eunice in the shoulder. "I know. I just needed to hear you say that!"

They went to the library and got *Polly Pitts's ABC's of Cookery*, which showed, in four easy steps, complete with color photos, how to separate an egg.

"Okay. Now. 'Incorporate with wire whisk. Be careful not to under- or overmix. Overmixing will produce a hard cake, while undermixing will result in large holes.' "

Their first cake rivaled the gingerbread that had chipped Mr. Gottlieb's tooth. The second looked like a minilunar landscape, complete with craters. The third, they decided, was good enough to test on Mrs. McKenzie.

Joy's mother might have named her only child Light of My Life if her husband hadn't insisted Joy was going far enough. She sat at the kitchen table, smiling proudly, as Joy set the slice of cake before her. At her first bite her tweezed eyebrows, which Eunice always imagined to be on little hinges, like windshield wipers, came crashing down above her nose. She stood and went to the sink, where she poured herself a large glass of water.

"It tastes wonderful, Princess," she said. "Just don't ever make it again, okay?"

"I had a feeling it was supposed to be higher."

"It said the layers would shrink."

"It said, 'slightly.' I think ours are more like 'drastically.'"

"Do you want to try again?"

"Does the sun rise in the east?"

"Butter."

"Butter."

"Sugar."

"Sugar."

"Six and one-half squares semisweet chocolate."

"We're all out."

"What? Already?"

"And it costs over two dollars a box, and we don't have one penny left."

Joy fingered her hairnet and frowned. "I'm not asking for an advance on my allowance. I'm just not. I don't want my parents involved."

Before Eunice could reply, the phone rang, and Joy leaped to it.

"Have Your Cake," she sang. She had already done this half a dozen times and each time had to explain coolly to one of her mother's friends or the dentist's receptionist what she was talking about. But this time, clutching the edge of her apron and snapping to attention, she went on, "That's right, the deluxe catering service, at your service." She grabbed a pen. "Yes, yes, of course. Tomorrow night? To serve twenty? No problem. Absolutely. Just let me get that address, Mrs. Ackeroyd. We'll have it there by five, I guarantee. Thank you. Bye-bye!"

She swung the receiver in a wide arc before putting it down, then pirouetted so many times Eunice had to grab the edge of the kitchen table to prevent herself from getting seasick.

"This is it, Eu! All it takes is one sale like this! Picture, if you will!" She grabbed a plate and fork from the drainboard, arched her brows, and exclaimed in a hoity-toity, la-di-da voice, "Why, Angela Ackeroyd, this is absolutely the most exquisite mousse I have ever tasted! I absolutely must have it for my next soiree! Wherever did you find such divine stuff? Have Your Cake? Ho-ho, what a delightful name! I'll ring them up at once!" Joy tossed her head and gave her surprising guffaw of a laugh—the only inelegant thing about her.

"Angela Ackeroyd? You mean Reggie Ackeroyd's mother?"

"None other!" Joy pliéd across the room. "If Ackeroyd likes us and if she recommends us to her friends—private lessons, here I come!"

Joy hugged her, mashing a vertebra or two. Built like a flamingo, the girl had the strength of a mountain gorilla. Eunice had to laugh too. They had never in their lives made mousse, they didn't have any money to buy ingredients, and they had an order from the mother of the richest kid in their school. Another chapter for the scrapbook!

Three

"NOW, EU, PLEASE, whatever you do, watch out for potholes."

"Joy, I haven't fallen off a bike since I was six years old."

"Okay, I know, I'm just so nervous. I wish we had a bottle of champagne to break against our fenders. Well, I guess this is it. Come on."

From their basements they'd each dug out the identical bike baskets they'd gotten for their eighth birthdays and attached little Have Your Cake signs. Each had a bowl of mousse. They'd borrowed the money for the ingredients from Millie, whom Eunice managed to catch just as she came in from a date with Richard, when she was still addled with kissing in the driveway.

"I wish we had uniforms," Joy said as they pushed off. "As soon as we buy those new pans, we'll get T-shirts, and then maybe little hats, for a real professional look. That's what small businesses have to do at first, plow every cent back into the enterprise."

The Ackeroyds lived in a Tudor-style minimansion on Fairmount. Eunice and Joy left their bikes out front and went around to the rear, where two long tables covered with white cloths were set by the built-in pool. A woman with dark, curly hair, wearing a long, rainbow-striped dress, was arranging vases of roses and ferns.

Joy cleared her voice. "Delivery from Have Your Cake."

The woman whirled around, setting her long copper and silver earrings swaying. In her ruddy, tanned face her smile was wide flash of white.

"I'll be! I thought you sounded young on the phone, but this is ridiculous."

Though insulted, Joy maintained her professional aplomb.

"Have Your Cake is an equal-opportunity employer and does not discriminate on the basis of sex, creed, race, or age. I'd advise getting this mousse under refrigeration, Mrs. Ackeroyd."

Mrs. Ackeroyd laughed merrily, and her earrings tinkled like tiny wind chimes. "I think I'd better take a gander at this mousse first. I believe your ad said satisfaction guaranteed?"

"Absolutely," said Joy, and only someone who knew her as well as Eunice did could have detected the twitch in her cheek. Eunice herself felt the sweat stand out on her brow and clamped her arms against her sides to ward off underarm wetness. Joy pulled the Saran wrap off one of the bowls of mousse, and Eunice held her breath. She and Joy had spent the last ten hours trying to come up with the World's, or at least Ohio's, Best Mousse. Nine and a half hours, to be exact. Mrs. McKenzie had insisted they take a half hour off for lunch. She had fixed them a tray of sandwiches which Eunice and Joy couldn't even bear to look at, they were so stuffed from taste testing. They felt the way they used to on Halloween night, when they sat on Eunice's front steps and ate their way through every 3 Musketeers and Milky Way they'd gotten.

But there it was, the fruit of their labor, the first product off the Have Your Cake assembly line. It looked wonderful. No one could have guessed, looking at it, that the McKenzies' garbage disposal had nearly self-destructed, trying to digest all the disaster mousse they'd dumped down it today. Eunice watched with bated breath as Angela Ackeroyd took a taste from the tip of her pinkie.

"Umm. Not the best I've ever tasted," she said. "But surely worth the price. Let's get it under refrigeration, Ms. McKenzie."

Through a supreme effort of will Eunice restrained herself from doing a handstand. Joy, her chin tilted toward the sky, gave a sigh that indicated her product had been insulted but that, it went without saying, the customer was always right. They followed Mrs. Ackeroyd inside through a sliding glass door.

The kitchen, all chrome and glass and gleaming tile, was in a mess that would have made Eunice's mother faint dead away. Mrs. Ackeroyd flipped a hand at the piles of clamshells, fish bones, and vegetable debris. "I'm doing all the rest of the cooking myself. I'm sure two chefs like you are familiar with bouillabaisse?"

"*These* are the *caterers*?"

In a corner of the kitchen, like a skeleton from the grave, Reggie Ackeroyd rose from the table. Her penetrating whine of a voice was pitched like a mosquito's. She herself was built like a dragonfly. Her orange hair was skinned up and spouted from a ponytail on top of her head. Her complexion was the color of boiled potatoes. Yet it wasn't just her looks that made everyone in Eunice and Joy's grade put her in a class with acid rain, poison ivy, and final exams.

"*These* are the *caterers*?" Reggie repeated when no one answered her. Eunice thought she saw Angela Ackeroyd wince, then quickly cover up with a smile.

"Yes, Regina, these *are* the caterers. Just look at the lovely mousse they've brought us."

But Reggie preferred to gawk at Joy, who, obtaining a platter from Mrs. Ackeroyd, unmolded the mousse exactly the way *Polly Pitts's ABC's of Cookery* showed. Behind Mrs. Ackeroyd's back she gave Eunice the high sign.

"But, Mom," whined Reggie, "they're in my class!"

"They are?" Mrs. Ackeroyd looked delighted. "What a happy coincidence!" She looked Eunice and Joy up and down, as if sizing them up for something.

"But they're just kids!" Reggie began to pull on her ridiculous plume of a ponytail, a gesture that made her mother reach over and grab her hand away.

"Regina, you'll be bald by the age of sixteen!" She turned and flashed that pearly smile at Eunice and Joy. "You're not *just* kids, are you? You're entrepreneurs, aren't you, Ms. McKenzie?" She patted Joy on the shoulder.

Eunice felt miffed that Mrs. Ackeroyd kept addressing Joy, yet she wasn't sure whether "entrepreneur" was a compliment or not. Joy, decorating the mousse with slivered almonds, gave the close-mouthed smile she reserved for small children and condescending adults.

"You can pay us now, Mrs. Ackeroyd, or we can bill you. I'm

sorry to say we can't accept VISA or MasterCard."

Angela Ackeroyd gave another one of her tickled-pink laughs, her earrings winking and swaying. "I'll have to run upstairs," she said. "You kids chat, have a Coke. I'll be right back."

Joy slipped the mousse into the refrigerator. From behind the kitchen table, where Eunice could see she'd been eating something mushy that had leaked onto the newspaper crossword, Reggie glared.

"You guys have a lot of nerve, deceiving the public," she said.

"So, Reggie, I see you've been taking charm lessons this summer." Joy ran a hand over a state-of-the-art food processor.

"You can get arrested for that, you know. False advertising. Get your hand off my mother's stuff. If that mousse isn't any good, you guys are gonna wind up in jail."

"If that mousse isn't any good, I'll dance naked in Higbee's window!" Joy hissed, then went on in her normal voice. "Were they expensive, the lessons? Maybe you could get your money back."

"Oh, you think you're so great!" Reggie sputtered, yanking at her ponytail. "You guys think you're so great, going around like twins all the time. Well, guess what? You're not."

"I wish I could locate these 'guys.' Have you had your eyes checked lately, Reggie?"

Reggie was about to erupt again just as her mother came sailing back into the room. Mrs. Ackeroyd frowned, then bit her lip. Reggie's scowl grew even more ferocious. Her mother turned away from her and handed Joy the money.

"That covers it, I think."

For the first time Joy looked flustered. "We don't have any change with us—"

"Never mind. You can put it toward my next order. I have a feeling this is the beginning of a long relationship." Drawing a breath, she turned back to Reggie and gently took her hand away from her ponytail. Still holding her daughter's hand, she asked, "Do you do cheesecake? It's one of Reggie's favorites, and she's got a birthday coming up. We want to make it very special. Don't we?"

Reggie pulled her hand out of her mother's and reached for the squashed sandwich lying on the table. She tore off a big bite. Red juice dribbled down her chin. Mrs. Ackeroyd put the back of her hand to her own forehead, and this time her laugh was tinny. "I'd better get busy, but you two stay and visit with Regina just as long as you like, hear?" And she hurried back out through the sliding glass door.

"No need to show us out, Reg," said Joy, making for the front door.

Eunice started to follow but turned in the kitchen doorway. Reggie, her scrawny shoulders slumped, stood staring after them, alone among the glass and chrome and fish bones.

"Good-bye," said Eunice, the first word she'd spoken the entire time.

Reggie gave a startled jump and then actually smiled. "Good riddance."

Joy was already on her bike, careering no-handed down the circular drive. "Come on," she said as Eunice caught up to her. "Back to the drawing board! We've got to learn how to do cheesecake!"

"I thought we'd go out and celebrate our first sale."

"We can't spend any of this money, Eu. I told you. We have to plow it all back into the business."

"I'll plow you."

"I guess we could share a small rocky road—"

"Aaargh! No more sugar! No more cream! I want a burger! I want fries! Grease and salt! Give me grease and salt!"

"Eunice, will you please keep your voice down? We're supposed to be gourmets, remember?"

Over their burgers Eunice asked Joy what entrepreneurs were. "Imbeciles."

"What? Mrs. Ackeroyd called us imbeciles and you agreed?"

"Shhhh! Do you always have to talk so loud?" Joy was peering past Eunice with a strange look on her face.

Eunice turned around. A group of boys and girls had come in. Eunice recognized them as ninth graders, a year older than she and Joy. The five of them—two boys and three girls—stood at the food counter, jostling one another, laughing, and generally looking around the place as if they owned it. A lowly seventh grader, who had been waiting a long time, quickly moved aside to let them go first.

"Imbeciles," said Joy again.

"Oh, them," said Eunice.

"Yes, them. Who else?" Joy dropped her voice to the barest whisper. "I wonder just who they think they are."

The group had gotten its order and now came down the aisle toward Joy and Eunice's booth. The three girls passed by Joy and Eunice first. One, in a halter top, cupped her fingers over her mouth and whispered something to the other two, who giggled with uncontrolled hilarity.

Eunice felt her teeth begin to grind. They couldn't have detected her BO; she'd plastered herself with Millie's Ban this morning. The girls plopped themselves down in a booth near the window, and the two boys slid in across from them. One of the boys, the one with dark blond hair, turned to throw Eunice and Joy a look. Somehow—how did he do it?—Eunice was instantly sure she had ketchup on her cheek, her shirt on inside out, or a bra strap showing. The girl in the halter leaned forward and said something that made the other girls all but slip off their seats and under the table, laughing. The boy with the taffy-colored hair threw them another look.

"For two cents I'd—" Joy broke off, unable to think of any fate drastic enough. "Who do they think they are?"

"Don't pay any attention to them." Eunice was surprised to see Joy so upset. It was rare that Joy let anyone get under her skin. Look at how she'd just handled Reggie. At school she wasn't even intimidated by the physically aggressive types who came barreling down the hallways, making it plain that anyone who didn't get out of their way was doomed to pancakehood.

Yet now she seemed unable to take her eyes off the group by the window, and Eunice begain to feel uneasy. "Remember what we always say, Joy. You and I are our own two-man crowd."

"Two-woman crowd," Joy corrected automatically, but Eunice could tell her heart wasn't in it. She tried to change the subject.

"I asked you what entrepreneurs are."

21

"What?"

"Entrepreneurs. What Mrs. Ackeroyd called us."

"Oh." Joy picked up her burger, which she had cut neatly in two and on which she'd ordered sliced tomato, hold the ketchup. Joy never ate junk food; an instrument of art deserved better. With an icy glance at the group by the window she explained, "They're movers and shakers. You and me, in other words."

This was more like the old Joy. Encouraged, Eunice went on. "Isn't it weird that Reggie's so obnoxious? When she has such a nice mother?"

Joy put her burger back down. "Who said her mother's so nice? Patting me like I'm a little pillow or something. Do you think she pats her hairdresser or her mechanic? We're doing a grown-up job; we deserve grown-up treatment."

"I don't know. She seems like the kind of person who just likes to pat everybody."

"I don't like people who pat. Anyway, I'm much more interested in the financial than the emotional angle of the Ackeroyds."

She never read "Dear Phoebe," either. It would be a waste of time to try to get Joy to speculate further on the root of Reggie's rottenness. Just then there was an earsplitting peal of laughter from the window booth.

"That does it," said Joy, standing up. She shot out the door, grabbed her bike, and was halfway to the corner before Eunice could catch up to her.

"Just remember," panted Joy, finally coming to a halt at the corner, "they fart just the same as we do."

This was an incredibly gross remark for Joy, who scorned all grossness. For an instant Eunice felt completely lost. Then she said, "Don't let them bother you! They're just imbeciles. You said so yourself. Don't pay any attention to them! Especially right now, at our moment of triumph with the Ackeroyds, and everything. We're our own crowd, right?"

"Right. Of course. I don't know what got into me. Probably food poisoning from that revolting burger." Joy tossed her head and tilted her chin toward the sky. "I'm recovered now. And we've got work to do. Even if Reggie is about as likable as a migraine, we're still going to bake her the most delectable cheesecake her mother ever tasted. Let's go."

She pushed off, and Eunice, with a fleeting regret for the revolting, delectable burger she'd left behind, followed.

Four

"ONE AND THREE-quarters cups fine graham cracker crumbs."

"One and three-quarters cups fine graham cracker crumbs."

"Eu, these are graham cracker *chunks*, not crumbs!"

"That's the crumbiest I can get them."

"All right, I guess they'll have to do. One half teaspoon cinnamon."

"One-half teaspoon cinnamon."

"One-half cup butter, melted."

"One-half cup butter—ouch!—melted."

"Springform pan."

"Springform pan. Are you sure this thing's going to work? It looks pretty tricky to me."

"Eunice, if you don't have confidence in us, who will? Five eight-ounce packages of cream cheese, softened. I said *softened!*"

"We must have missed the line about leaving them at room temperature one to one and a half hours."

"All right, they'll have to do. Three eggs. One cup sugar. Beater. Here we go."

The beater, which belonged to Mrs. Gottlieb and which Eunice had sneaked over to Joy's house, made a noise like a rhino stuck in quicksand. Within seconds foul smoke had begun to fill the room. Joy pushed the beater up to its highest speed, and the machine, completely coated with claylike cream cheese, whined in anguish. She shook it and stamped her foot.

"Joy! Turn it off, quick! If it breaks, I'll be grounded till I'm twenty-one!"

Joy switched the beater off, and Eunice grabbed it just before she threw it on the floor.

"We can do it by hand. People must have made cheesecakes before they invented beaters, right?"

By the time they'd gotten the thing in the oven Eunice was sure she'd permanently dislocated her arm. She was also afraid that the beater, which her mother had gotten for a wedding present and always bragged was indestructible, had been put permanently out of commission. That meant she, Eunice Enid Gottlieb, would be too.

But when the cake came out of the oven, it looked so beautiful, so completely, dazzlingly professional that she forgot everything else.

"There it is," whispered Joy rapturously. "The perfect cheesecake, on our very first try."

Ever so gently, neither of them breathing, she loosened the sides of the springform pan. It worked. The cake stood there in all its creamy glory.

Joy and Eunice shook hands. They pounded each other on the back. They asked each other whoever said baking was tricky. They turned, beaming, to admire the cake once more.

And then, down the very center of the cake, a huge crack appeared. As they watched, it split the cake neatly in two.

"I wonder if the Galloping Gourmet ever feels like crying," Eunice said slowly.

Joy didn't answer. Instead, she crossed the room, came back, and handed Eunice the box of graham crackers.

"One and three-quarters cups fine graham cracker crumbs."

"One and three-quarters cups fine graham cracker crumbs."

Five

TWO DAYS LATER they got their next order, again for mousse, from a Mrs. Lizzie Benson, who had attended Angela Ackeroyd's dinner party and received Have Your Cake's name with the highest of recommendations. A few days after that Charlotte Hippenhammer called to inquire whether they could handle a rush order for that very evening? Her good friend Angela Ackeroyd had assured her they could do anything they set their minds to.

"I told you she was nice," crowed Eunice as they zoomed around Stop 'n' Shop, grabbing up chocolate and cream.

"I wonder what's in it for her," said Joy, diving for a place in the express line.

"Faith in humanity isn't one of your strong points, Joy."

"I've told you before—it comes from being an only child. If you'd spent as much time around adults as I have, you'd be on the lookout for ulterior motives all the time, too."

"Well, anyway, we're getting orders. That's the main thing."

"Right. Tomorrow we'll go down and get our T-shirts made. Between word of mouth and our big ad in this week's paper, the phone should be ringing off the hook. I bet I'll be able to start private lessons by mid-October." And right there in the express line she stood on her toes, spun around twice, and hugged Eunice so hard Eunice thought she heard a rib crack.

The next day was Saturday. Eunice, who slept on the second floor with Millie, woke up feeling hot and sticky. The heat wave the forecasters had predicted had arrived. From downstairs she could hear her mother's voice, and it sounded very crabby. Mrs. Gottlieb, whose crabbiness quotient was probably about normal for a working mother, couldn't tolerate heat. Eunice decided to stay in bed awhile longer.

But before she could even turn over, there was a pounding on the stairs, and Russell came flying across the room to land on her stomach.

"See, I told you! For your information, gorillas do not eat kittens!"

"I'll eat *you!* Get off me, you flake!"

But Russell was holding a *National Geographic* in front of her nose. The magazine was his favorite reading material. He was always begging someone to take him to the library so he could check out another stack of back issues. Now he pointed triumphantly at a photo of a gargantuan mound of black hair cuddling a tiny green-eyed kitten.

"See?" he said. "Gorillas are vegetarians, it says right here. And it says they're often gentle to smaller creatures, in the wild, too, not just in captivity. It's their true nature. It's natural. So you can tell Joy she was wrong."

Eunice had all but forgotten about the gorilla and kitten photo in the newspaper and how Joy had pronounced the whole thing unnatural. Now she tumbled Russell off her and took the magazine from him. Inside was a series of pictures: the gorilla trying to soothe the kitten, which looked pretty nervous about all this. The two of them playing. And there in the final picture the kitten, looking drowsy and contented, nestled right in the gorilla's lap. The gorilla wore a very tender expression. *Tender* was the only word for it, though it was probably the last word one would think to apply to a gorilla. Ferociously tender, and grateful too. What a loony, mismatched pair! They made Eunice think of those early American paintings of a lion and a lamb lying down together. Weird, certainly. Fairy taleish. Yet somehow not unnatural. There was a moral to the photos, and though Eunice wasn't sure what it was, she did know they were very nice pictures to wake up to. If everyone looked at photos like these first thing in the morning, the world might be a better place.

Eunice reached over and tousled her brother's hair. "I'll tell Joy," she said.

"Don't forget, okay? I bet she's been worrying and worrying about that kitten."

"Eunice Gottlieb! Do you intend to sleep away the entire morning?" Their mother's voice, coming from the foot of the stairs, made Eunice think of barbed wire.

"Uh-oh," she said.

Russell rolled his eyes. "She's making one of her lists. She's got chores for all of us to do. You're supposed to take the kitchen chairs out in the driveway and scrub them."

"Yikes. It must really be hot out." Eunice, who slept in a T-shirt, got out of bed. Today definitely called for what Joy termed the Path of Least Resistance. She pulled on a pair of shorts, poked Russell in the belly, and, in the Houdini-like move she'd perfected over the years, slipped down the stairs and out the front door before her mother could catch her.

Joy had dance class that morning, so Eunice, after being polite to Mr. and Mrs. McKenzie, who were on their way out to do Saturday-morning errands, settled into phone duty alone. Their new, improved ad listed call-in hours, to make sure they didn't miss any orders. Joy said someday they'd get an answering machine. Eunice flipped on the radio that sat on the kitchen counter, just in time to catch the weather forecast. This, the man predicted, was only the beginning of an unusually torrid summer. Eunice groaned and snapped off the radio. It wasn't just her mother's crooked big toe that she'd inherited. Eunice couldn't tolerate heat either. There was no doubt that in her previous life she'd been a polar bear.

And this year the heat would bring a new problem. Just standing there in the McKenzie kitchen, doing absolutely nothing, Eunice was sweating. Buckets. Well, teacups anyway. Definitely thimbles. Horrible! What did her body have against her anyway? All these years they'd been on such good terms, and now it had turned on her like this. Thank goodness she and Joy had this business together, to make the summer tolerable.

Eunice opened the refrigerator and let the cold air waft over her. On the bottom shelf sat their latest cheesecake. It was, they both agreed, their best yet. No crack. Graham cracker crumbs instead of chunks. The only problem was the way the whole thing sort of caved in toward the center. If you ate it with your eyes closed, though, it was perfection. Eunice decided a cool, melt-in-the-mouth slice was just what she needed to beat the heat. She was on her way back for her third slice when the phone rang.

"Have Your Cake!"

"Ms. McKenzie?"

"No, this is . . . Ms. Gottlieb."

"Oh, how are you? This is Angela Ackeroyd!"

What a jolly voice she had, for an adult! No heat wave could slow her down; she sounded as peppery as ever.

"Fine, thank you. How are you?"

"Oh, just peachy! How's business?"

"Great—thanks to you!" Eunice was immediately glad that Joy wasn't there to hear her gush with such unprofessional gratitude.

"No, no—no thanks to me. I've merely recommended you; it's your mousse that's winning you customers! But Ms.—do you mind if I call you by your first name?"

"No, that's okay. It's Eunice."

"Eunice! Really? I had a dear, favorite great-aunt named Eunice! She crocheted us all our own antimacassars when we got married. But, Eunice, what I called to ask was—Regina's birthday is coming up next week. She's going to be thirteen, you know. Such a milestone! It deserves a very special cake, don't you think? Now—I hope you won't be insulted—I was wondering if I could get a gander at your cheesecake before I order it."

No one had ever asked that before. What would Joy say? Eunice looked down at the piece she'd been eating.

"I guess so. I mean, that would be fine. Would you like me to bring it out to you?"

"Oh, could you?"

"When do you want me to come?"

"Is now at all convenient?"

"I'll be right there, Mrs. Ackeroyd."

"*Angela*. Thanks so much, Eunice! Bye-bye!"

Eunice was halfway there before she realized she'd abandoned the phone during call-in hours. What if Joy called and no one answered? *I'd never have done it for anyone else,* Eunice would explain, *but we owe something to Angela. Yes, she told me to call her Angela!* Joy would have to be impressed to learn she'd gotten on a first-name basis with such a wealthy, influential client.

No one answered the front doorbell. After walking around to the back, Eunice found Reggie just climbing out of the pool. Her marmalade-colored hair was plastered to her skull, and she wore a two-piece, blindingly orange suit that was a grave mistake. Reggie wrapped herself in a monogrammed towel and hopped from one foot to another as if she were freezing, though it was at least ninety degrees.

"My mother's not here."

"But I just—"

"She got beeped."

"Huh?"

"One of her patients needed her, dummy."

Eunice hadn't known Angela was a doctor. The knowledge made her breezy, friendly manner all the more amazing. Eunice thought of her own mother, who usually came home from her job as a Tempo office worker so worn out she could hardly even talk till Russell fixed her a glass of her favorite instant iced tea.

"I didn't know your mother was a doctor."

"She's a radiotherapist." Reggie made a zapping sound and shot a hand toward Eunice's face. "She X-rays people."

"I had an X ray once, when I was six years old. I fell off my bike, and they thought I had a concussion."

"Not that piddly kind of X ray. For cancer and yucky stuff like that. My mother saves people's lives, dummy."

"Do you mind if I put this cheesecake in the refrigerator? She can call us after she tries it."

"Suit yourself."

Eunice started toward the sliding glass door. Behind her she could feel Reggie hesitate and then scurry along. Inside, it was blessedly cool: central air-conditioning. The kitchen gleamed, nothing like the shambles it had been the night of Angela's dinner party. From upstairs came the sudden roar of a vacuum cleaner.

"I thought you said your mother wasn't home!" Eunice cried accusingly.

"That's the housekeeper, dummy. You think my mother would waste her time cleaning? Mrs. Sterling takes care of the house. And she's supposed to make sure I don't drown. As if she'd care."

On the kitchen table were a crossword puzzle book, a can of Hawaiian Punch, and two glasses, as if Reggie were expecting a guest. As Eunice put the slice of cake—she'd cut it with great care so the cave-in wasn't so obvious—in the refrigerator, Reggie stood dripping beside her. Her lips were the color of blueberries.

"The cake's for my birthday, you know."

"I know."

"It's going to be a really big party."

"Oh, yeah?" Eunice started to move toward the front door.

"That's my big sister, so don't bother to ask."

Eunice hadn't even noticed the oil portrait Reggie jerked a thumb at. The large-eyed, ivory-skinned girl with the cloud of red hair was Reggie if she'd aged a few years, gained at least fifteen pounds, and had a beauty make-over. Yet the way she smiled, serene as a cat in the sun, but playful, too, was pure Angela.

"I didn't know you had a big sister."

"That's a switch!" Reggie snorted and tugged on her ponytail. "Most people say they didn't know she had a little sister! She's in medical school in Boston. She's going to be a neurosurgeon. Everyone in my family's brilliant, you know." Reggie, who was by no means known for her grades, pulled on her ponytail so hard Eunice saw the skin at her temples turn bright pink.

"When I'm sixteen, I'm getting my portrait painted too. It costs at least a thousand dollars, but that's nothing to my mother. She'd pay a million for me." She wheeled around to face Eunice. "You have a big sister too."

"No kidding."

"I'm just making conversation; you don't have to sound so snippy."

"Me!" Eunice once more started for the door. "Tell your mother to call me about the cheesecake."

"Does she talk to you?"

Eunice turned around. Reggie was pulling furiously on her ponytail, and Eunice had a flash of how Russell used to suck his thumb and twirl a lock of his hair when he was tired or upset. "Who? Your mother?"

"No, dummy. Your big sister."

"Listen to me, Ackeroyd. Lay off calling me dummy, understand?"

She smiled! She actually smiled! The girl was clearly demented.

"Okay, okay! Just tell me."

"Of course, she talks to me. We live in the same house; we sleep in the same room—how could she not talk to me?"

"You sleep in the same room?" *You eat fried rat?* was what her incredulous tone implied.

"You've never heard of people sleeping in the same room before?"

"When my sister comes home on vacation she has her own suite on the third floor."

"Well, my sister says when she leaves home, she's never coming back." Somehow this didn't come off as the crushing retort Eunice had intended it to be. Reggie, wrapped in her enormous monogrammed towel, hopped from one foot to the other and grinned.

"I've always had my own room."

"If that's the best thing you can think of to brag about, you're in trouble." What was she doing, standing here, trading insults with this mosquito? Eunice pulled open the massive front door and was blasted by a blowtorch of afternoon heat.

"I'm not bragging. It's just a fact of life." Reggie hopped up and down in front of the painting of her sister. "It must be really yucky to have to share a room and not have any privacy. It must be a real big drag."

"Not as bad as having a sister so much smarter and prettier than you!"

Eunice hadn't meant to be so extreme. It was the heat, coupled with that insistent dentist's drill of a voice. Reggie stopped hopping, and her big towel drooped, showing one sticklike, goose-bumped arm.

"So long," said Eunice, heading out the door. "I have to get back to the office."

"The office!" she head Reggie say as she picked up her bike. "Ha-ha—I'd like to see your office! You and Joy think you're so great! Stuck together like circus freaks all the time!"

The last words were swallowed up in a little gulp that echoed in Eunice's brain all the way back to Joy's house.

Six

OF COURSE, WHEN Joy got back from dance class, Eunice had to describe the entire scene.

"I didn't mean to be so mean to her," she concluded.

"Mean? Egad, the girl has to come face-to-face with reality. She's a creep!" The McKenzie kitchen had swivel chairs, and Joy, pushing off from the table with one bare foot, spun herself around. "I'd say you did her a favor, teaching her she can't treat people that way." Joy spun again, making Eunice light-headed.

"But you'd think she'd have learned that by now. She doesn't have one friend in the whole class."

Joy spun again. "You just feel guilty. Your mother's drilled politeness into you till it's as second nature as nit-picking to a monkey."

"I can't imagine what it'd be like to be so alone."

"You're the one who admires how Dear Phoebe always lays it on the line, right? If Reggie has no friends it's her own fault. Now stop grinding your teeth, okay? You look like Attila the Hun." Joy reached for a peach from the bowl on the table. "That's great work, getting on a first-name basis with Angela. Oh, Eu!" She suddenly stretched her long arms above her head so her hair spilled over the back of the chair and the peach glowed above her like a tiny sun. "Dance class was so good today! I'm coming into my prime. I can just feel it! I can't wa-ait for those private lessons! And that reminds me." She lowered her head, and her tone became abruptly unpassionate. "I think it's pretty important for us to be at the phone during advertised times, if we're going to seem professional."

"I know. I just thought for Angela . . ."

"Okay, okay. Anyway, call-in hours are over now. Let's go to the pool."

She ran up to her room and came back sucking the peach pit and wearing last year's faded bathing suit. Though Joy regarded her body as an instrument of art, she never paid any attention to the clothes she put on it. If Eunice had gone around in the kind of stretched-out, frayed clothes Joy did, she'd have looked like a bag lady in training. But not Joy. Nothing could hide her loveliness. In her junky clothes she was exactly like a masterpiece in a decrepit old frame.

Joy scribbled a note to her mother, and they rode to Eunice's house.

"The pool?" said Mrs. Gottlieb, who was peeling hard-boiled eggs. Eunice could tell right away, from the way she was smacking the eggs on the edge of the counter, that her mother was going to give her a hard time.

"First you disappear this morning without a word about where you're going. Now you waltz in here and say you're headed for the pool. I don't suppose it ever occurred to you this is more than just a boarding-house." Mrs. Gottlieb wiped her brow with the back of her hand and demolished another eggshell. "I don't suppose it ever occurred to you I might need some help around here."

"Mom, I was out on business."

"This family is your business, Eunice. What would happen if your father and I just came and went as we pleased, with no concern for the rest of you? What would happen then?"

"That's different. You—"

"I want you to take the kitchen chairs out in the driveway and scrub them down."

"Mom, it's twelve thousand degrees out! They're warning people to avoid physical exercise!"

"Then you're bringing your little brother to the pool with you. He's been mooning around the house all day alone."

"Blackmail! Who'd have thought my own mother would stoop to it?"

"Eunice, stop that fresh talk or I'll change my mind." Whack! went another egg.

With a grimace at Joy, who sat on the living room rug, stretching her hamstrings, Eunice went to her brother's room. He was lying on his bed, perfectly content, reading yet another issue of *National Geographic*.

"Put on your suit, Russ-o. You're going to the pool."

He sat up, his dark eyes wide, his cheek crinkled and pink where it had rested on the bedspread. "Guess what? The whole world used to be one piece; then it got broken."

Eunice drew a deep breath and prayed for strength. "We're in a hurry," she said.

He sat up, unfolding a map entitled "Earth's Dynamic Crust." "See, here's South America and Africa and wow! Even Antarctica, all snug as bugs. And there's the United States—I mean, North America, tucked right in there too." He jabbed the map with a grubby finger.

"Russell, this is summer vacation. No more social studies, okay?"

"This isn't social studies; this is real life! It says these plates or something—I can't exactly understand it, but it's because there's a fire in the middle of the earth—these plates started messing around, sliding all over the place, and wow! That must have been pretty scary! A whole continent just floating away, bye-bye! It must have seemed like the end of the world for sure!"

"Where's your bathing suit?"

It only took him fifteen minutes to find his suit, another ten to put it on, and then what seemed forever to receive his mother's instructions on staying with Eunice, not running in his flip-flops, using his sunscreen. . . .

"Mom, the pool will be closed by the time we get there."

"And make sure you buy something nutritious to eat, not junk," said Mrs. Gottlieb, handing Eunice some money. "Be good and have fun."

As if you could do both at the same time! Her first day at the pool this summer and she was showing up with her brother in his Smurf swimsuit, his nose a pyramid of zinc oxide. Thank goodness she and Joy weren't the kind who cared what other people thought about them. Thank goodness they were their own two-woman crowd, no matter what.

The pool was jammed. The three of them dropped their towels across from the high dive, and Joy immediately ran around to the board.

Eunice didn't know how to dive. She eased herself into the water from the side. She always thought of this moment as letting herself into another world. The water was a calm, silent place where she could feel both graceful and strong. It curved around her and held her up; it trailed along her body like gentle, cool fingers. A person could become part of the water world in a way she never could lose herself on land. Sometimes, when she was swimming, slipping under and breaking through the sunlit sparkle of the surface, Eunice felt as if she might turn into something else and be only a little surprised.

Now she did a little sidestroke and watched Russell, his stubby lashes all spiky and his face solemn with his dog paddling. Why had she made such a stink about bringing him? He was no trouble. Nothing was any trouble. Everything was just as it should be. And to think the whole summer lay ahead, a cool, shining river that would flow who knew where—

"Whoa!" cried Russell. "Just like on *Wide World of Sports!*"

Eunice looked up in time to see Joy bounce, touch her toes, and slip into the water as neatly as if it had parted for her. Russell raised his hands to clap, and sank. Joy was back up on the board in a flash, the little kids who couldn't do anything fancier than a cannonball making way for her with awe. This time she did a half somersault and slipped into the water again so cleanly there was barely a sound. Next to dance, Eunice knew, diving was Joy's great love. "I just enjoy defying gravity," she often explained.

Now Joy dived so many times, and always with such exquisite precision, that Eunice grew exhausted watching her. She climbed out of the pool, leaving Russell to his placid dog paddling, and stretched out on her towel. The air was heavy with the familiar summer smells of chlorine and coconut oil. Someone's radio announced that at the end of the first the Indians were losing, 7-0. Her poor father. Just last night he'd taken Russell to watch the team stretch its losing streak to nine games. "Your father has always been loyal to lost causes," her mother said. Eunice opened one of her word-finder puzzle books. She wasn't going to think about her mother or Reggie; she wasn't going to let anything spoil this perfect afternoon.

But as she opened her book, she noticed the boy.

He was the same one who had turned around to stare at them in the burger place. She recognized his tangled honey blond hair and his dark eyes. He was sitting at the edge of a group of ninth-grade boys and girls, and even though he sat with his arms loosely draped around his drawn-up legs, there was something coiled about him, like a spring in a box. He was staring at Joy. As she climbed and dived again and again, he watched intently, even though he had to squint straight into the sun to do it. He had dark lashes, so long they brushed his cheek. He didn't pay the slightest attention to what the others around him were doing, even when one of the girls slapped a palmful of sunscreen on his bare back.

Watching him watch, Eunice thought the sun had begun to dim, as if some heavy thundercloud were skidding across the sky toward the pool. Watching him watch, she began to feel the same uneasiness she had when Joy burst out with that remark about farting. She opened her book to a puzzle called "Zoo Time" but couldn't even concentrate enough to find *ape*.

At last Joy climbed out of the pool and, with a toss of her head and a tug at her bleached-out old suit, came toward Eunice. She was going to have to walk directly in front of the ninth graders. Eunice closed her book. The boy let his hands fall onto the cement behind him, but didn't take his eyes off her. Joy, beaming, was waving at Eunice. The diving had put her in such ecstasy she was oblivious of his staring, or she was deliberately ignoring him. Either way it was amazing. Joy was truly the rarest of . . .

She stumbled. Just as she passed him Joy, who never, ever, lost her balance, stumbled.

"Are you okay?" asked Eunice.

"What?" Joy grabbed up her towel.

"You tripped."

"I did not," she snapped. "Anyway, if you'd been diving for forty-five minutes your legs might be a little unsteady too."

"If I'd been diving for forty-five seconds you'd have to peel me off the bottom of the pool."

"Call Russell. Let's go."

Eunice stood up and saw that the boy was still watching. Now that he wasn't squinting, she could see that his eyes were exactly like black stars.

Seven

DEAR PHOEBE:

I was very happily married for eight years. Then I discovered my husband was having an affair with his dumb blond secretary. I gave him a choice: her or me. He chose her.

This was three years ago. I continue to believe my husband will wake up one morning and realize he has left a decent, loving woman for one with a geranium in her cranium. I am so sure of this that every night I set two places at the dinner table in case this is the night he comes back.

My friends have begun to hint that I have gone around the bend. I say they don't know the meaning of the word *loyalty*. Who is right?

FAITHFUL FRAN IN EVANSTON

DEAR FAITHFUL:

Yes, loyalty is a virtue. However, like all virtues, it can be carried to an extreme. Then it becomes unhealthy.

You said it yourself: He chose her. Painful as that is to face, you must, if you are going to get on with your life. Get professional counseling. And good luck, dear.

Eunice, sitting in the McKenzies' kitchen, held the paper close and peered at Dear Phoebe's photograph. Always that same smiling face and that perfect hairdo. She must use a case of hair spray a day.

Eunice folded the paper and laid it on the kitchen table. What made her think a thing like that about Phoebe, whom up to now she'd just about worshipped? It must be the heat. Still, Eunice couldn't help wondering how someone who came, day after day, face-to-face with the Real, Unwhitewashed World, could keep her hair so neat. In every photo Eunice had ever seen of her, and the two times she'd seen her live on TV, Phoebe's hair had been just as smooth and sleek. You'd think she'd tear it out. Or at least run her hand through it a couple of times.

Joy had a cello lesson today, so Eunice was again on phone duty. It didn't bother her, since when Joy was busy, she had nothing to do anyway. Yet the day was even more of a scorcher than the one before, and the phone didn't ring. It was so hot that the smallest action required a monumental effort, and it seemed to take about ten years to walk across the room to the refrigerator. But Eunice made it and ate some mousse that had turned out too thick. She thought of the Ackeroyd's house, with its central air-conditioning.

The phone rang.

"Have Your Cake!"

"If you want our order, you better come out here right now."

There was no mistaking that voice like a nail on a blackboard, yet Eunice pretended to be confused.

"Excuse me? Who's calling please?"

There was a sputter, and she could just see Reggie reaching for her ponytail.

"Do you want our order or not? It's for two cakes, one with and one without strawberries. I'm allergic to strawberries. I'm very sensitive."

"Is this, by any chance, the Ackeroyd residence?"

"Don't pretend with me! We're probably the only people who ever order from you!"

"I can take your order over the phone, Ms. Ackeroyd."

"Oh, no, you can't!"

"Why not?"

"Because—because my mother wants you to come out here, so she can discuss the details. These cakes are for my birthday, you know. They're the most important thing in the world to her."

Eunice threw a glance at the clock. Fifteen minutes till call-in hours ended. What Angela wanted, Angela got.

"I can be there as soon as the office closes."

"Well, make it snappy."

As soon as Eunice hung up, the phone rang again.

"How's business, partner?"

"Booming! I'm on my way out to the Ackeroyds' again, to get their cheesecake order."

"She's making you come all the way out there? Who does she think she is, the queen of Persia?"

"It's a double order, Joy. I don't mind."

"I tell you, I don't trust her. But that's beside the point. The point is she's buying from us. Which brings me to my next question."

There was a pause, during which Eunice could hear the screech of a tormented stringed instrument in the background.

"I'd like to have a brief business meeting, okay? Meeting called to order." Joy cleared her throat. "I have a motion to put before the board. I move we give our executives a small advance on the profits. Does anyone second the motion?"

"Huh?"

"I think it's about time we paid ourselves. We deserve it."

"I've been saying that all along."

"Then just say, 'I second the motion.'"

"I sec—"

"All in favor say aye. Aye."

"Aye."

"Motion carried. How about twenty dollars each?"

"That much? We'll be wiped out."

"Do you think John D. Rockefeller got rich by being cautious? He didn't know the meaning of the word! But of course, I respect your opinion. How about fourteen ninety-five?"

"What if we suddenly get a bunch of orders? We won't have enough to buy supplies! And we need another springform pan."

"Egad! You're on your way over to the Ackeroyds', aren't you? Don't you have any faith in us?"

"Sure, but—"

"Just get her to pay today."

"Okay."

"I won't be home till late. Call you tomorrow morning."

As she rode over to the Ackeroyds', Eunice felt as if she'd swallowed something indigestible. It was not, of course, the first time Joy had talked her into doing something against her own judgment; what bothered her was that paying themselves so much money was totally unlike Joy. It didn't take a degree in accounting to see that exhausting the business's capital all at once not only was unprofessional. It was plain dumb. What could Joy want the money for? What could be so important? And Eunice realized that this was what really troubled her: Joy hadn't been completely honest. Her best friend was keeping something from her.

It *was* the first time for that.

"Hey, where do you think you're going?"

The inimitable whine brought Eunice to herself, and she realized she was riding right past the Ackeroyds' house. As she turned back and rode up the circular drive, she saw the orange plume quivering in the doorway.

"The big-time caterer's here."

Eunice parked her bike and stepped into the wonderful coolness, expecting Angela to come striding toward her with her brilliant smile. But the entrance hall was empty, and the house silent.

"She got beeped again."

The way Reggie pulled so frantically on her ponytail and avoided Eunice's eye made Eunice suspicious. Well, she wasn't putting up with this today. Turning on her heel, she said "Tell your mother to call me."

"Where are you going?" shrieked Reggie. "She told me to make the order. She gave me the money and everything!"

"Okay, give it to me then."

"Come on in the kitchen."

A middle-aged woman in a pale blue uniform was unloading the dishwasher. When Reggie introduced her, Mrs. Sterling gave Eunice a shy smile.

"That's nice you got a friend, Regina," she said. She put the last dish on the shelf. "Now I'm going to take my break and put my feet up. You be sure and tell me if you decide to go in that pool." She poured herself a cup of coffee and left the room.

Reggie jerked open the refrigerator door. Taped to the outside was a big appointment calendar. Every day of July was scribbled full in what Eunice was sure was Angela's dashing handwriting. Reggie got out a can of Hawaiian Punch and poured two tall glasses.

"You want a marshmallow Snow Ball?" She reached two packages down from a cupboard.

"No, thank you."

"You can have the pink one." Reggie set them on a plate before her.

"You're ordering two cheesecakes?"

"On account of my allergies. I have all kinds of yucky allergies. I break out in these huge yucky—"

"Let me give you some advise, Reggie. Cut out the 'yucky.'"

Reggie, her mouth full of Snow Ball, widened her eyes.

"It's a fourth-grade word. You sound ridiculous using it. Now when do you want these cakes?"

Reggie washed down her Snow Ball with a slug of Hawaiian Punch. "Do I really?" she asked, almost quietly. "Sound like a fourth grader?"

"Well, maybe a fifth grader. Anyway, you should cut it out of your vocabulary." She watched Reggie thoughtfully cram the rest of the cake into her mouth. "When do you want us to deliver?"

"Come around six. We gotta go to the airport to get my sister. She's flying in for the party."

"Fine." Eunice stood up. "I hope your mother really gave you some money because on a big order like this we need payment in advance."

"First you have to go in the pool."

"What?"

"My mother said you have to take a dip in our pool."

"She did not."

"My mother's a very generous person. It makes her unhappy not to share her stuff. She said I had to make you go in the pool." Reggie tore a bite out of the other Snow Ball.

"You're nuts."

"You can wear one of my sister's old bathing suits. And if you don't, I won't give you the money." Reggie sprinted out of the room toward the stairs.

"I'm not going swimming!" Eunice yelled after her.

"You don't have anything better to do on a hot day like this!" Reggie screamed back.

Eunice stood alone in the kitchen. As soon as she left this house the melted iron of the afternoon sun would pour down on her head. Without Joy she had no place to go but home. Her mother, not working today and no doubt on the verge of heat stroke herself, would want to know what was wrong and why she was so moody. When Eunice said, "Nothing," she'd reply that work cured all ills and dream up some chore. Scraping crud off chair legs. Polishing the gravy boat they used twice a year. Ironing the kitchen curtains with their endless ruffles.

Eunice headed up the stairs.

Reggie stood on the landing, holding a green suit. "You can change in the bathroom. I never let anyone except my closest friends in my bedroom."

Whom did she think she was fooling? She had as many close friends as the moon had trees. Eunice went into the bathroom. The soft jade green suit (that was the color suit Reggie should have worn, instead of orange) was too tight on the bottom and hung in empty pleats on top.

Eunice, looking like a combined ad for the Grapefruit Diet Plan and Pounds On, followed Reggie downstairs.

"We're going swimming!" Reggie yelled in the general direction of the living room.

"All right, Regina," said Mrs. Sterling.

Reggie slid open the glass doors.

"Last one in is a rotten eggplant!" she shrieked, and sprinted toward the pool. She catapulted off the side, splashed down, and came up gasping. Thrashing her way back to the side, she taunted, "Rotten eggplant, rotten eggplant!"

In and out in ten seconds, to satisfy this creep, who had now added blackmail to her list of endearing qualities.

But the instant Eunice slipped into the water she knew she was going to have to stay awhile. The cool, pure water, the quiet so deep she could hear the breeze ruffling the leaves and a cardinal singing—how could she ever have enjoyed the public pool, with its near-lethal level of chlorine and its screaming, splashing mob? Reggie's pool had no ropes, no lanes, no rules. It was surrounded by tubs of scarlet geraniums. Swimming here was like swimming in the sky. Sky, water, Eunice—-all were the same warmth and all shot with sun. She swam through drifting clouds and red flowers.

"You're a good swimmer!"

The water must have distorted her hearing. Eunice found Reggie desperately treading water beside her.

"What did you say?"

"I said, 'You're a good swimmer.'"

"Thank you."

"Isn't it a beautiful pool?"

"Yes."

"Everyone who comes here says it's the most beautiful pool they've ever—" She got a mouthful of water. "Sppp! Most beautiful pool they've ever seen."

"Oh yeah?"

"What do you mean 'Oh yeah?' Don't you believe—" But Reggie seemed to run out of steam. Maybe the pool's peacefulness charmed even her. She said. "I swim here every day."

"I don't blame you."

Reggie paddled to the side of the pool and hung on. "My mother built it just for me and my sister. The coach on the high school swim team told my sister she could be in the Olympics if she wanted."

"It's nice of her to come for your birthday."

"She's not coming for my birthday. She couldn't care less about my birthday."

Eunice saw at once Reggie hadn't meant to say that, but now that it was out, she was so stupid and ornery she had to go on.

"My sister doesn't like me. She's jealous of me, is what it is. Because—because now she's gone, I get all the attention."

"Then what's she coming to your party for?"

"Because. Because my mother's making her come."

Eunice considered that this was possible. It would take a strong person to resist Angela's will.

You want to come?"

"Huh?"

"Are you deaf or something? I said, 'You want to come?'"

"To your party?"

"No, to Mars."

Reggie, by clinging to the side of the pool, managed to give her ponytail a yank.

"I—well, I mean, thanks a lot. But I don't think it would be very, you know, professional to attend a party we were catering."

Reggie didn't even blink, and Eunice guessed she had never in twelve thousand years expected Eunice to say yes. Hastily Eunice pulled herself up out of the water.

"Speaking of professional, do you know what time it is? I have to man the phone," she lied.

Reggie raised her bony wrist. "Half past a freckle, Eastern elbow time."

"Ha-ha-ha, that's a good one."

Reggie stared at Eunice with a directness that made Eunice flinch and start for the house.

"You don't have to come in. I can just change real quick. Thanks a lot for the swim."

Reggie didn't answer. Eunice hurried through the arctic-aired house. Mrs. Sterling's vacuum roared in some distant room. She draped the jade green suit carefully over the shower curtain bar and went back out into the blistering afternoon.

She was almost home before she remembered she hadn't gotten the money from Reggie. Have Your Cake's bank account was just about mopped. Well, she'd leave her own $14.95 untouched, that was all.

The thought made her feel queasy again. What did Joy need that money for? Was she in trouble? Did she want something so silly she was embarrassed to tell Eunice about it?

Tomorrow, first thing, I'll ask her.

Eight

"YOU'RE ON YOUR way to sit by that phone all afternoon again?" Millie actually tore her eyes away from *All My Children* for one entire second. Beside her on the living room floor Russell was pushing around blobs of Play-Doh, frowning and muttering to himself. "When does Joy get her turn to do some of the work?"

"Joy has her tennis lesson this afternoon," Eunice said.

"How convenient." Millie's eyes swung back to the TV.

"Her mother makes her." Eunice, planning to ask Joy about the $14.95 the instant she saw her, was pleased to have this chance to display her faith in her best friend. "Mrs. McKenzie insists on Joy becoming well rounded. She makes her take cello and French and art and—"

"Sit down," said a woman on TV. "I'm afraid you're in for a shock."

Millie risked darting another glance at her sister. "I'm just wondering. It doesn't seem to me your division of labor is very fair. And as your number one stockholder I have a right to my opinion."

Did she actually care, or was she just trying to be bossy? Eunice could never be certain, since Millie, depending on how her love affair with her flake boyfriend was going at the moment, wanted one day to smother Eunice with big-sisterly affection and the next to smother her, period.

"I've always loved Craig!" someone on the TV sobbed, having one of the hysterical fits that came every three minutes. "Nothing you can tell me will change that!"

"Go for it!" Millie yelled at the screen, then said calmly to Eunice, "In other words, how come you're stuck doing all the work?"

"I'm not. Joy has provided ninety-nine percent of the brainpower."

"Getting something done is one percent inspiration, ninety-nine percent perspiration. No offense."

"And besides," said Eunice, "we're best friends. Best friends don't keep tabs like that." She thought of the red and white scrapbook, bursting with mementos of all they'd shared. Even goofy old Russell, poking at his Play-Doh—once, aeons ago, they'd decided Joy would marry Russell, so they could be truly related and live together forevermore. She rushed on. "With best friends everything evens out in the end."

"And you, my child, are extremely naïve!" The woman on TV wept.

Millie fell to her knees. "I knew it!" she cried, wringing her hands. "Craig's been cheating on Donna!"

"And by the way, Millie, I hate to tell you, but the surgeon general has just issued a warning: Watching soaps causes brain shrinkage."

"The dirty rat! The scum! After all she's done for him!"

Eunice strode out of the room. In the kitchen, on the stove, was a note from her mother, who had been called in to work today.

MILLIE

Start pork chops at 4:30, 350 degrees.
Peel potatoes well.   Make sure Russell doesn't get overheated. Make sure he has MILK, not Kool-Aid, for lunch.

EUNICE

Hereupon Eunice abruptly ceased reading, so she could honestly report to her mother that she hadn't seen her instructions for the day.

"All I'm doing," said Millie, appearing in the doorway (Eunice could hear the commercial), "is trying to give you some advice."

"If I need advice, I'll write to 'Dear Phoebe.'"

"You know I like Joy. But it's a natural human tendency to get away with as much as you can."

The soap came back on. Millie took to her heels but called over her shoulder, "I'm just trying to look out for you, you schnickelfritz! Whether you believe it or not!"

As Eunice let herself into the McKenzie kitchen, the phone was ringing. Grabbing her pencil, she took an order for a cheesecake from Angela's friend Liz Benson and had barely replaced the receiver when Charlotte Hippenhammer was ordering one, too. A half hour later a new customer called, saying she'd heard a rumor their mousse was the best buy in town.

Eunice yelled to the empty kitchen, "Wait till Joy hears!" To celebrate, she helped herself to a dish of strawberry glaze and heavy cream.

Of course, there was the small matter of how they were going to fill the orders, since they didn't have enough money to buy ingredients. But Eunice wasn't worried. "Don't you have any faith in us?" Joy had demanded, and look how right she'd been. The business was taking off! Once they got over this small hurdle, they'd be rich. And once she and Joy had had one of their heart-to-heart talks, everything would fall into place. She went into the living room to watch out the window for Joy.

She didn't come. She was a half hour late. An hour late. Eunice got more and more worried. What if Joy had injured herself on the tennis court? Or if something had happened on her bike ride home? After an hour and a half of waiting, during which she distractedly took one more order, Eunice was considering calling Mrs. McKenzie at work when she saw Joy wheel into the driveway, a small pink parcel under her arm.

"Where *were* you? Are you okay?"

Joy cradled her package against her chest. Eunice recognized the name of a high-priced department store in a nearby mall.

"You went shopping? Why didn't you call me? I've been waiting and waiting!"

Joy looked at the clock, blushed, and looked confused. "It's that late? Do you think it's too late to go to the pool?"

"The pool! Are you crazy? We don't have time to go to the pool! Look at this, Joy." Eunice held up the list of order. "Four, count 'em!"

Joy looked at the list as if it were hieroglyphics. Eunice began to read orders aloud. "Mrs. Liz Benson, one strawberry cheesecake. By the way, I think we'd better start substituting blueberries; they're cheaper than strawberries now. Mrs. Charlotte Hippenhammer, one—"

"Super, super!" Joy waved her hand as if shooing away a pesky insect. "But listen, there's no way we can start cooking now. My mother will be home soon, and you know she draws the line on our baking while she's getting supper. Let's go to the pool. I'm so hot from that inane tennis."

"But"—Eunice spoke slowly—"but you've just spent the last hour and a half in an air-conditioned mall. I'm the one who's been sitting here in the heat."

"Then it'd be good for you, too, wouldn't it? Come on, just one quick dip." Joy picked up her pink package. "You can wear one of my suits." She ran up to her room and came back down with a T-shirt over her suit. She threw a faded old suit at Eunice and sped on out the door.

Joy pedaled so fast Eunice thought her heart would burst, trying to keep up. *And how,* gasped her mind, *how is it that for the second time in two days you're going swimming when you don't want to, in a suit guaranteed to make you look awful?*

Joy had already rented the locker and was throwing her shoes into it when Eunice caught up. Eunice sank onto a bench.

"Joy," she said, after she'd gotten her breath, "before we go out to the pool, I need to talk to you. I have something to ask you."

"I have something to ask you too." Joy had been fingering the hem of her T-shirt, and now she suddenly whipped it off over her head. "What do you think?"

She was wearing a brand-new bathing suit. It had skinny little straps, soft gathers down the front, and was hot pink. It was, unmistakably, a bathing suit for someone who thought her body an instrument of beauty. And who wanted everyone else to think so too.

"What do you think?" repeated Joy, tilting her chin. "Do I look okay?"

Eunice was struck dumb in triplicate. Number one because Joy had bought such a bathing suit in the first place. Number two because she was obviously anxious and unsure about it. And number three because Joy had breasts.

There they were, on either side of the hot pink gathers. Not big. Not what anyone would call buxom. But undeniably there. Where had they come from? They hadn't been there in May, when Joy, in a simple black leotard, had given her dance recital. They hadn't been there a month ago, the last time Eunice had slept at her house. They hadn't even been there two days ago, when Joy had given her diving exhibition. Along with all the other amazing accomplishments of her life, Joy had managed to grow breasts overnight.

"Are those falsies?"

Eunice!" Joy hissed furiously, and looked around to see if anyone had heard. "How can you even suggest I'd do anything so gross as . . . egad! Me?"

"You look so different."

"Am I supposed to take that as a compliment, or what?"

"You're acting different too. I never saw you care so much about how you looked."

"Just tell me if it looks okay."

"You know you look beautiful."

Joy's face relaxed. "Thanks."

"You're welcome."

"I agree it's not my usual style. Something just came over me." She draped a snowy towel around her long, lovely neck. "You should get a new suit too. Something with vertical lines."

"Huh?"

"I've been meaning to tell you, you'd better stop snacking on our rejects. Come on."

Eunice, wearing the stretched- and bleached-out suit Joy had worn two days earlier, followed her out of the locker room. It was possible Joy had actually had breasts two days ago; in this suit a girl could have Miss Teenage America's body and no one would ever suspect. When they stepped out into the sudden sunlight, Joy's new suit gleamed sleekly. The air all around her seemed to shimmer with a rosy, iridescent glow. To think she could have looked like this whenever she wanted but had never bothered. Why did she want to now? What had changed her? Joy began climbing to the high dive. Eunice, in the castoff suit, felt the way she had two days ago, as if she'd swallowed something indigestible.

Of course. There was the $14.95. Supplemented by several weeks' advance on Joy's allowance, no doubt. She wouldn't ask her parents for money for the business, but she would for that suit.

Joy gave a small expert bounce on the end of the board and then—how did she do it?—sailed down through the air, like a pink blossom blown loose in a breeze.

And Eunice, feeling as if she, too, were moving in slow motion, turned to look across the pool. There he was, immobile as a cat watching a bird.

Joy dived; Eunice and the boy watched.

At last the lifeguards blew their whistles to clear the pool for a rest period. Eunice realized she hadn't even gone in. Joy came walking toward her, pink and sparkling in the late-afternoon light. She was going to walk right in front of him again. She could have gone around to the other end of the pool, but she didn't. Here she came. There he was.

He said something.

Eunice saw his lips move. She saw Joy flick him a look, move her own lips, and keep on walking.

She didn't stumble. But when she sat down beside Eunice, she was trembling.

"What did he say?" Eunice asked.

"Who?"

"You know who!"

"He said hi. Very profound."

"What did you say?"

"I recited the Gettysburg Address. What do you think I said? I said hi back."

"You could have told me that's why you wanted an advance on our salaries. To buy a new suit."

"I really did need a new one. That one you have on is revolting."

"So why didn't you just come out and tell me?"

"You never asked." Joy examined the extraordinarily high arch of her left foot. "Is he looking at us?"

"Yes."

"I thought so. I can feel his eyes. Only a perfect cretin would stare like that."

"You won't have to put up with him for a while anyway." Eunice talked fast, as if her words could push back the cloud sliding across the sun. "We have so many orders we won't have time for the pool. We're really going to have to work. Once we figure out how we're going to buy the ingredients, that is."

Joy stood up, her back still toward the boy, and stretched. "We'd better go. I forgot to leave my mother a note; she'll have the National Guard out."

"Didn't you hear what I said? Mrs. Hippenhammer wants her cheesecake tomorrow."

"How about borrowing from Millie again? We could pay her back, as soon as Mrs. Hippenhammer pays."

"I guess—I guess I could ask her."

"She'll say yes. I know you don't believe it, but she likes you. Only one thing: I have my museum class till eleven tomorrow. Do you think you could do the shopping without me?"

Eunice stood up, trying not to remember what Millie had said about her doing all the work. "I guess so."

Joy threw her arms around Eunice's shoulder. "Partner," she said, and they turned and walked back toward the locker room. Ever since they were little, ever since the jack-o'-lantern photo, when they both were missing front teeth, they had liked to walk with their arms around each other's shoulders.

They passed behind the boy, who turned to stare.

"A perfect cretin," muttered Joy, but as they went into the locker room, she missed the step, and stumbled.

Nine

EUNICE'S TIMING WAS impeccable. She caught Millie just as she came in the side door that night. Richard had taken her to a health food restaurant and whispered sweet nothings over seaweed and mashed yeast. Millie's eyelashes had uncurled, but her cheeks were pinched pinker than ever.

"Eunice, you know what it's like when a shower is so hot it makes you shiver?" Millie sighed. "That's what being in love is like."

"Can I borrow ten dollars?"

Money in hand, Eunice rode her bike to Stop 'n' Shop the next morning. She was already throwing things into the Mixmaster mixing bowl when Joy came home, lugging a huge drawing pad.

"Guess who I saw at the museum?"

Eunice mopped her brow with a dish towel. "Who?"

"Ackeroyd, all by her emaciated self. Our teacher took us down to the Oriental section, and there she was, slithering around in the gloom like some kind of ghost. She jumped ten feet in the air when she saw us and took off. A sad case. What should I do? The graham cracker crumbs? Egad, it's the Mojave Desert out there. As soon as this is done, we'll reward ourselves with a dip."

"We can't go to the pool." Eunice told herself her knees felt weak because of the heat. "We have a mousse to do after this, and we have to deliver Hippenhammer's cheesecake."

But Eunice had forgotten how, when Joy wanted to, she could get anything done in half the time it took an ordinary mortal. Bing bang boom, purée whip chill, they had the cheesecake cooling in the oven and the mousse setting in the refrigerator.

"Are we amazing or are we amazing?" Joy chugged a glass of club soda and swiveled her chair.

Eunice mixed herself some chocolate milk. "We have two cakes on Saturday for Reggie's birthday. As Dear Phoebe always says, good luck has a partner: elbow grease."

Joy set her glass on the table and jumped out of her chair. "And now for a cool dip."

Eunice stopped stirring her milk. "But we have to de—"

"I know, I know! *After* we deliver the cheesecake."

"But I'm not sure the cake's cool enough. You know we decided that's what makes them crack."

"It won't crack." Joy was already on her way up to her room to change. "And if it does, we'll say that's how it's supposed to be. We'll say it's our special trademark."

Eunice put the cake in one of the white cardboard boxes they'd bought at the bakery supply store and loaded it into the new wide wire basket on her bike. When Joy came out the back door, she saw that instead of her Have Your Cake T-shirt, she was wearing a short, floaty white robe, like a sprinkling of sugar over the hot pink suit.

"It came with the suit," she said, as defensively as a child explaining a kitten that had followed her home.

"You cannot deliver a cake wearing that."

"Right. I'll wait around the corner while you deliver it. Here, I brought down my old suit so we won't have to bother going past your house."

"How thoughtful of you."

Joy, about to push off on her bike, paused at Eunice's tone.

"Joy, you yourself said that suit's revolting."

"You're right, I'm sorry."

Eunice, who knew she was the only person on earth Joy ever apologized to, felt a little better. They stopped at her house for her suit and then rode to the Hippenhammers', where Joy, in her see-through cover-up, hid behind the high boxwood hedge while Eunice delivered the cheesecake.

Almost positive the cake had cracked by now, she prayed that Mrs. Hippenhammer wouldn't open the box. But when she didn't and, instead, fishing her wallet from an enormous purse, exclaimed how heartening it was to see young people being so industrious and making such productive use of their summer, Eunice didn't feel relieved. She felt like a crook.

"We should have given her a discount," she said to Joy.

"Caveat emptor."

"What's that mean?"

"What you see is what you get," quoted Joy, and began her breakneck race toward the pool. In the locker room, while Eunice changed into her suit, she used the open locker door as a barre and did exercises, as if warming up for a performance.

"Are you going to spend the whole time diving again?"

"Do I detect an undertone of hostility here?" Joy arched her brow and did five pirouettes. "You're awfully ornery today. The heat's bad for you, Eu. If you lived in a tropical climate, you'd probably turn into a mass murderer."

Enice, clutching her towel and her word-finder game book to her front, followed Joy out to the pool. The boy was there again, and as soon as Joy appeared, one of his friends nudged him in the ribs and began to laugh. The boy gave a slight smile and ducked his head. Joy, without one glance in his direction, headed for the board. Eunice just stood there. She felt on the verge of something but didn't know what. It was like having a word on the tip of her tongue. She tried and tried but somehow couldn't say it. . . .

"Who does she think she is, God's gift to the universe?" The screech came directly in her ear, just as Joy dived. "What a show-off!" whined Reggie Ackeroyd, whom Eunice turned to find beside her in all her flaming orange glory. "I wonder who she thinks she is!"

"She doesn't have to think who she is," retorted Eunice with automatic loyalty. "Joy knows exactly who she is."

"She must think she's the only one who knows how to dive. I can dive like that, too, you know. My mother got me and my sister private lessons. But you won't catch me putting on a show for the whole pool."

Joy was already back up on the board. The boy's friend nudged him again and laughed. Some girls in the crowd were looking toward her and Reggie, and Eunice realized they must be thinking she and Reggie were friends. She dropped her towel and book and jumped into the water, abandoning Reggie in mid-whine.

Eunice had never been able to understand people who did laps, plowing the water instead of playing with it. But now she did them, furiously, back and forth across the width of the pool until one more stroke was impossible. She hung, exhausted, on the edge of the pool. Joy had to be finished diving by now.

She was. She was right there, in the spot she and Eunice had claimed for themselves the past few days. Only now she was standing talking to him.

Detached from his friends, he looked smaller and less sure of himself. He also looked unbelievably handsome. No one that good-looking could have a brain in his head. Joy had undoubtedly been right: All that staring had been a symptom of mental defectiveness. Just look at how he was hanging on her every word! As she spoke he leaned closer and closer. He seemed about to lose his balance; he seemed, in fact, about to fall flat at her feet.

No time to waste—Eunice had to rescue her best friend from this nitwit.

She climbed out of the pool and started toward them.

But then something happened. Joy turned her head slightly, and Eunice knew she'd seen her approaching. But instead of smiling with gratitude, Joy frowned and flicked her wrist, as if brushing off a mosquito.

Eunice stopped. To say the ground seemed to slip out from beneath her would not have been exaggerating. What could Joy possibly mean?

"We have to find a place in the shade. I get sun poisoning."

Eunice wheeled on Reggie.

"What are you talking about?"

"You can get convulsions from it and swallow your tongue. Once I got these big blisters—my mother almost had a nervous breakdown, she was so worried. There's some shade by the wading pool."

"I'm not sitting with you!"

"You're not? Then who are you sitting with?"

Eunice turned to see Joy and the boy moving off toward the snack bar.

"She thinks she's so great!"

Eunice gave Reggie a look. If looks could kill, Reggie would have needed an ambulance.

Then Eunice turned and fled to the locker room.

Ten

"COOL IT, DEAR," Dear Phoebe counseled Green-Eyed Monster in Minneapolis.

"Sam is a two-timer and a creep," she declared to Can't Sign This. "Wake up and smell the coffee, honey."

"You have made a bad mistake," she announced to Desperate in Dubuque. "But remember this: Life is no egg. Its pieces can always be put back together."

Sitting on the edge of the bathtub, Eunice gazed across Millie's forest of shampoo bottles. What all of Dear Phoebe's advice boiled down to was this: Life is hard. People are cruel. Treachery lurks where you least expect it. Here was the Unwhitewashed Truth: All too often the only helping hand you'll find is at the end of your own sleeve.

She'd been reading "Dear Phoebe" for so many years, you'd think she'd know that. But here was another truth she hadn't suspected: Awful things didn't happen only to other people. Awful things could happen to you.

Knock knock knock!

"Beat it! Scram! Leave me alone for once in my life!"

"Fine. Is that what you want me to tell your friend?"

Eunice unlocked and flung open the door. "What friend?"

Millie shrugged, heading for the phone. "I may be enough of a sucker to lend you money, but I'm not your social secretary."

"Okay, okay, I'm sorry." Eunice rushed past her into the kitchen and grabbed the phone. "Hello?"

"Eu, what happened to you? I turned around and you were gone. His name is Robert Gray. Doesn't it sound like a poet's name?"

"Robert . . ."

"He doesn't let anyone call him Bob. If someone calls him Bob or Robbie, he sets the person straight immediately."

Joy recounted this with the breathlessness she usually reserved for Twyla Tharp's latest choreography.

"He's highly principled," she said.

"He's too good-looking."

"How can anyone be too good-looking?"

"Isn't he conceited?"

"I don't know." Joy gave a laugh Eunice had never heard before, not her usual guffaw at all. It was the laugh equivalent of a pirouette.

Eunice leaned against the kitchen sink. First Joy had transformed herself to look like a stranger, and now she sounded like one. Eunice felt the way she did when she was in water deeper than she'd thought, tried to touch bottom, and couldn't.

"Well," she said. "So. What now?"

Joy spun another laugh. "What are you sounding so serious about? So—we talked. He's in ninth grade, and he plays soccer. His birthday is March third, a Pisces, just like you."

"Pisces, ha. He can't even swim."

"Of course he can swim."

"Then how come all he ever does is sit?"

"Tomorrow I'm going to introduce you. I need your evaluation."

"Tomorrow? Tomorrow we have to make Reggie's birthday cakes, and Mrs. Benson's, and deliver—"

"Egad, Eu! Didn't you ever hear the expression 'All work and no play makes Jill a dull girl'?" The exasperation in Joy's voice—Eunice had a flash of her gesture that afternoon, the flick of her wrist that had made the ground slip away.

"Listen, Joy, this business was your idea." Her voice, which she wanted to sound stern, trembled.

"What's that supposed to mean?"

"I—I don't know." Eunice felt herself floundering, panicking, the bottom not there.

"I just called to tell you about Robert. Exactly as I've told you every other thing of any importance in my entire life."

Eunice drew a deep breath. Maybe nothing had really changed after all.

"I thought you'd want to know about him, Eu."

"I do. Of course, I do. But—"

"Ackeroyd will get her precious birthday cakes, no sweat."

Eunice felt some trickle down her own armpits. Where had Joy gotten that expression?

"Okay? So don't worry about the business."

But that's not what I'm worried about.

"Okay."

"Okay. Au reservoir!"

"Au reservoir."

Eleven

JOY CAME WINGING home from dance class the next morning, and together they baked Reggie's two birthday cheesecakes. Joy was in such a rush she didn't even bother to change out of her purple leotard. When they were finished, she still looked as cool as plum ice.

"I hope you brought your suit," she said, "so we won't have to stop by your house."

"I brought it. But I'm not sure I'm in such a hurry to get to the pool."

"How many times do I have to tell you: Don't be so resistant to new things! Don't you know that's why the dinosaurs died out?"

"Because they weren't popular? They died of hurt feelings? Is that what you're telling me?"

"Who said anything about popular? I just want you to meet someone I think is interesting, that's all."

"I won't fit in, Joy. I don't know how to talk to kids like them. Besides, I'm shaped like a potato pierogi. I can't sit there half naked with *them*."

"Just be yourself. 'This above all . . .'—remember? I'll be right there, just like always. Now come on."

But as she followed Joy out of the locker room, Eunice felt her entire body shift into clench. Even her eyelashes were tense. The boys and girls in Robert Gray's group were in their usual spot; who would dare try to take it from them? They might as well have built an electrified fence around their square of poolside, for all anyone who didn't belong with them would risk intruding. Joy headed straight for them, self-possessed as a fire walker.

As soon as he saw her Robert Gray leaped to his feet. He moved his towel a foot or so away from the rest of the group, and Joy spread hers beside it. Together they made their own small island just off the larger continent.

"Robert, this is my best friend, Eunice Gottlieb."

"Hey," he said.

Eunice tried to smile, and she must have managed at least a reasonable facsimile because Robert Gray gave her a quick nod and sat back down. Joy sank beside him.

Eunice just stood there. What was she supposed to do? There was a small strip of space between Joy and another girl. Should she ask the girl to move? But she didn't know her. She didn't know any of these people. What if the girl just ignored her? Or even refused? Though she had taken a shower at Joy's and drenched her underarms with Mrs. McKenzie's deodorant, Eunice began to sweat. The girls, she knew, were all inwardly smirking at her, hulking there over them like a gigantic lost child.

"Sit down," came Joy's voice. She moved her towel closer to Robert. "Or maybe you should go in. You look on the verge of heat stroke."

Does she really care? Or is she just trying to get rid of me?

"Eunice is an excellent swimmer," Joy was telling Robert, who smiled his Clearasil ad smile.

"Hey, that's great," he said, and Joy beamed at the profundity of this remark.

Eunice would have given anything to be in the water. Submerged. Hidden. Away from all these curious, mocking eyes. But going in the pool meant taking off her T-shirt. Everyone would watch. They'd see her chubby, babyish body up close. Every other girl there had a waistline. And they all had breasts. Not a pierogi among them.

At last she managed to sit down. Yet the longer she sat there, the worse she felt. Everyone was talking, but not to her. How could they think of so many things to say? Even if she'd been able to come up with a remark worth remarking, her jaw felt as it if were wired shut. Joy, she could see, was too new to the group to introduce her to the other girls or even to talk to them herself—not that she gave the slightest indication of wanting to. All her attention was reserved for Robert, who was telling her he'd made JV soccer this year. Joy listened raptly. Eunice remembered a film she and Joy had once watched on the late late show, where invaders from space had hollowed out people's skulls and put in something resembling peanut butter. She tried to imagine Robert Gray with green skin and antennae sticking out of his head; but sitting in the middle of this group, she was the alien, and everyone knew it. Oh, a few of the girls smiled at her, but just like piranhas, all you saw was teeth.

On the edge of the group was a short, skinny boy who kept cracking his knuckles and trying to get attention by making loud remarks sprinkled with four-letter words. His voice, like his knuckles, kept cracking, and every once in a while one of the girls would good-naturedly tell him to shut up and give him a little shove. This made him go on louder than ever. Eunice thought of Reggie. *At least I'm not a fool,* she told herself.

Robert was still talking. He was describing a new music video. Eunice had seen it, too, and thought it was disgustingly violent. Joy listened with a perfectly bland expression on her face, and Eunice thought it was just the way some people listened to music: ignoring the words, only hearing the melody.

"I hated it," Eunice blurted.

Robert and Joy both turned to look at her, obviously having forgotten her existence.

"Hey," said Robert. "You did? How come?"

"It was sexist, and it exploited women."

"Hey, I guess it did. I didn't think of that." He nodded, pretending to be thoughtful. Solemnity made him handsomer yet, like one of the Greek statues Joy sketched at the museum. "Are you a feminist or something?"

"Eunice is Eunice," said Joy, and though this was finally her chance to include Eunice in the conversation, that was all she said. She just sat there, smiling at them both.

"I saw the girls' soccer team play last year. They were pretty good, for girls," said Robert.

Joy lay down on her stomach, and he immediately flattened himself beside her. Their faces cradled in their arms, they lay smiling at each other, as dim-witted as characters on Millie's soap.

I don't have to sit here, Eunice telegraphed to her legs, but the longer she sat, the more impossible it was to move. She could feel herself turning into a damp, sweaty stone. If she got up and walked away, everyone would see Joy had dropped her. Abandoned and betrayed her. They all would see that the only reason Joy had insisted on Eunice's coming here today was to ease her own conscience, so she wouldn't have to face the fact that she'd tossed away her lifelong friend as carelessly as her old, bleached-out bathing suit. Eunice smiled harder yet.

"Do you like soccer?"

One of the other boys had actually spoken to her. Eunice tried to move her parched lips.

"Sucker?" she croaked.

Somebody laughed. Eunice felt her baked stone face break up into separate and uncontrollable pieces; her forehead tightened, her eyes burned, and the smile she'd been holding for what seemed forever went skittering straight off her face.

"Let's get her!" one of the boys shouted, and in an instant they all, including Robert Gray, were on their feet. They rushed toward a girl in a ruffled turquoise suit. One grabbed her arms and the other her ankles, and they began to haul her, wriggling and screaming, toward the pool.

"No horseplay!" blared the lifeguard through her megaphone. "No horseplay!"

The knuckle cracker kept trying to get in on things and being jostled away. They threw the girl into the pool and then came racing back toward him.

"Okay, Woody Woodpecker! Your turn!"

But they'd only begun to chase him when the lifeguard started climbing down from her stand. One of the boys picked him up, spun him around over his head, and dropped him in an ignominious heap. Then they all dived for their towels and sat smiling innocently as the lifeguard threatened to throw them out if they didn't watch it.

"Hey!" said Robert Gray. "No sweat! No sweat!"

The girls, sniffing and sneering at the boys, took their towels and moved a few feet away. Only Joy remained, calmly waiting for Robert to return to his senses and her side.

Woody Woodpecker surreptitiously examined a scrape on his shin. If both legs had been broken, he'd have kept on grinning. Coming back up to the group, he called the lifeguard a name. From the hopeful look on his face it was obvious he thought now, at last, he might become one of the crowd.

No one paid him the slightest attention.

Eunice stood up. "I'll deliver the cakes," she said. "You don't have to bother to come."

Joy looked up. Here was the most clear-cut moment of all, when, if one shred of their old friendship remained, she'd cry, "Egad! You know we're *partners!*"

"Thanks, Eu," said Joy. "You're a true friend."

And search as she might, Eunice couldn't find a trace of guilt in her face.

Twelve

EUNICE RODE STRAIGHT to Joy's house, boxed the two cakes, and loaded them onto her bike. She took all the rejects too. Except for the file box of recipes, there was no trace of their partnership when she left.

At home she set the supper table without her mother's having to nag her, then took a shower and changed into her Have Your Cake T-shirt. When Millie saw her, she said, "I see you're still doing all the work. I suppose Joy is off at a lesson, getting well rounded."

A vision of Joy's breasts rose before Eunice's eyes. A couple of years ago Joy had heard that lying naked under a full moon made breasts bloom magnificently, and of course they'd had to try it, sneaking out of Eunice's room in the middle of the night. They had gotten covered with magnificent mosquito bites. Eunice could feel their itch that very moment.

"What are all these boxes doing in my refrigerator?" Mrs. Gott-lieb was demanding in the kitchen.

"It's for the business," said Eunice.

"Since when is my refrigerator for rent? Russell, I'm not calling you again! Eu, please get him."

Russell sat at his desk. Taped up next to the photo of the gorilla and the kitten was the *National Geographic* map showing how the world had once been whole. Russell was working away at his Play-Doh, singing, "And on this farm he had a cow, GI, GI Joe!"

"Russell, come eat supper."

He turned around. "Yikes, Eu. You're as red as the mid-Atlantic ridge!" He pointed to his map.

But instead of the map, Eunice looked at the photo of the gorilla cuddling the kitten. It didn't look so natural anymore. Russell swore gorillas didn't eat kittens. But how could he be so sure? Life was hard; people were cruel; treachery lurked where you least expected it. Eunice wouldn't have been the least surprised if the next issue of *National Geographic* related how the gorilla had popped that little kitty like a salted peanut.

In the kitchen Mrs. Gottlieb took one look at Russell's hands and told him to go wash off the Play-Doh.

"That's not Play-Doh; that's Africa."

"You go wash it off. Eunice, what's wrong? Take a wiener."

"I'm not hungry."

"Nonsense," said her mother, forking a frank onto her plate.

"It's suppertime," admonished her father, who believed in schedules as sincerely as he did in underdogs.

"I'm not hungry."

"Look, Mrs. Miller's piccalilli, your favorite," said her mother.

"I'm not hungry."

"Maybe she has sun poisoning," said Millie. "Look how red she is."

"Want some of my Oxnema?" offered Russell again.

You were heartsick, and they offered you hot dogs and Noxzema.

"Speaking of the Millers, I finished that birdhouse for them this afternoon," said Mr. Gottlieb.

"Wonderful. I don't suppose you noticed that while you were making birdhouses for the neighbors, our grass has grown six feet tall?"

"We're all hot, Doris. Don't take it out on us."

"And don't take it out on me because the Indians lost again."

Your world had fallen down around you, and they went right on with their petty bickering.

"What's for dessert?" piped up Russell.

"Dessert?" Eunice said. She jumped up and went to the refrigerator. "Here." She plopped a reject cheesecake on the table. "Eat this."

There was a collective widening of eyes. Even Millie looked mildly impressed. Eunice realized none of them had ever seen a Have Your Cake product. She laid big slices on four dessert dishes.

"You made this?"

"You don't have to sound so amazed!"

"But . . . it's delicious! And it's so professional!"

"It's as good as Sara Lee!" said Russell.

"It's a million times better, dolt!" said Millie.

Eunice didn't know what to say. Their compliments took her completely by surprise. They each seemed as proud as if they'd baked it themselves.

"Doris," said her father, "you're going to have to start taking lessons from your daughter."

"You're just saying that because you're always for the underdog," said Eunice, cutting everyone seconds.

"One thing I'll say for your father. He can't tell a lie, even a white one." Her mother reached for the plate Russell was holding in two hands and licking, then came and hugged Eunice from behind. Her voice grew soft, for what seemed the first time in weeks. "We're proud of you, you schnickelfritz. You've really done something here."

"And all on her own," added Millie.

Their approval was like balm on blistered skin: It couldn't heal, but it soothed. Mrs. Gottlieb didn't even remind Eunice it was her turn to do the dishes. Russell walked her out to her bike, carrying one of the cakes. Millie, who'd gone upstairs to get ready for her date, called down from the window, "It's Richard's birthday next month. Maybe I'll order a cake from you—provided you give me a discount."

Riding toward the Ackeroyds', Eunice thought: *Here it is again, the "Gottlieb Family Yo-Yo Effect."* Joy had come up with the term one day as Eunice was complaining that just when her family was driving her the craziest, when they had, in her opinion, outdone even the most outrageous stuff in "Dear Phoebe," they turned around and did something nice. Joy had nodded solemnly. "Your family pushes you to the limit, then zap! reels you back in again.

From this we can conclude that they never really mean to hurt you. They're just blunderers, which is par for the human race."

How many times had Joy hatched Eunice's thoughts for her? Given definition to a muddled mess of anger or confusion? Millie had once told Eunice not to let Joy think for her, but Eunice knew she didn't. Joy had only helped Eunice make sense of her life. And she in turn had been the one person prickly, suspicious Joy really trusted.

"This above all . . ." But her life was so entwined with Joy's. Without Joy, how could Eunice even know who the self she had to be true to was?

Thirteen

THERE WAS NO answer at the Ackeroyd front door, so Eunice wheeled her bike around to the back. Big bunches of balloons hung from the trees near the pool, and a banner that read LUCKY 13TH!!! fluttered in the evening breeze. As Eunice put down her kickstand, the sliding glass doors opened, and Angela, in a white, embroidered caftan, came out with her arm around the waist of the girl in the hall portrait. She wore a jade green dress, and her long red hair was loose on her shoulders. Something she said made Angela throw back her own curly dark head and laugh, setting her heavy silver earrings swinging. As Eunice watched, she pulled her daughter to her in a quick, hard hug. A tall man with an immensely high forehead followed them, carrying a bottle of champagne on a silver tray. When he spoke, it was in a booming baritone.

"The cake woman cometh!"

Angela whirled around. Throwing out her arms and flashing her wide smile, she flew to Eunice.

"If it isn't my favorite caterer!" she cried, and kissed Eunice on the cheek. She was so gleeful that her usual vivacity seemed like sleepwalking by comparison. She took Eunice by the hand.

"This is José, my Latin lover from New Jersey." She pronounced it "New Joisey," and José took a deep, starched bow. "And this—this, Eunice, is my older daughter, Lydia!" She buried her face against Lydia's neck.

"Mom, will you calm down?" Lydia wriggled away, smiling and rumpling her mother's hair. She held out a hand to Eunice, and Eunice, shifting cake boxes, managed to hold out one of hers. Lydia gave it a firm, hearty shake. Her hand seemed very strong for someone so slender, and Eunice remembered Reggie had said she was going to be a neurosurgeon. These fingers pressing hers would one day be digging around inside brains. . . .

"So you're Reggie's new friend! Mom's told me how much Reggie enjoys your company. And you run a catering service all by yourself!"

"Well, no, you see, actually—"

"Here, have a stuffed mushroom." Angela plucked one from the dish José had just brought out and held it to Eunice's lips.

"No, thanks, I just had supper. I'm just here to drop off—"

"Do us a favor, Eunice!" José boomed in a voice that would have qualified him for the Metropolitan Opera. "The stuffed mushrooms are just the tip of the iceberg. There's spanakopitta, shrimp on toast, a cheese ball big enough to feed New Joisey, and who knows what else."

"Yes, please, Eunice, I got carried away." Mrs. Ackeroyd took another mushroom from José and popped it in Eunice's mouth. "Lydia has that effect on me!"

Eunice, her arms full of cake boxes, had no choice but to open her mouth and let Angela pop in half a dozen more mushrooms.

"I'll open the champagne!" proclaimed José.

"Hurry up!" said Angela, plying Eunice with shrimp. "Any moment now that phone will start ringing, and it won't stop the whole time Lyd's here. The instant word goes out she's in town, the hordes descend." She hugged Lydia again.

"Calm down, Mom," said Lydia.

"It's your fault. If you'd come home more often I wouldn't act so nutsy!"

"You would too. You can't help it. You're just an exclamation point with legs, that's all."

Mother and daughter grinned at each other, while José, making some remark in Spanish that set them all three laughing, peeled the foil from the champagne bottle. Though Lydia wasn't as nutsy as Angela, she was exactly the daughter you'd expect her to have: handsome, charming, obviously in charge of her life. Now they had their heads together, serious expressions on their faces, talking intently. Eunice could imagine them that way all night, talking and talking like two girlfriends. At dawn they'd come out here to the garden, disheveled and groggy and beautiful, to watch the sunrise. Now they broke away from each other, and Angela rushed around urging food on everyone, bubbling nonsense. Eunice felt as if she'd tuned into Millie's soap at one of the rare moments when things were going well and the characters' joy was complete. José was still fumbling with the champagne, Angela was laughing at his clumsiness, and Lydia smiled at them both lovingly.

In Eunice's experience sublime family moments like this one came very rarely and lasted ten minutes, at the outside. Then her father made a remark that set her mother off, or Eunice sat in bubble gum, or Russell choked on something. But right now these three were enclosed within a glass bell that shot prisms in every direction. They seemed, clustered there, capable of sustaining happiness forever.

"There's some stupid creep on the phone!"

Whack! Smash went the crystal bell. Reggie tottered in the sliding glass doorway, wearing a yellow minidress and high-heeled yellow sandals. Eunice could almost see Angela count to ten before she turned and said, "Creep? We don't know any creeps, Regina."

"He wants to talk to Lyd, and he won't say who he is. 'It's a surprise!'" she mimicked, her voice rising. "I call that a creep."

"It's probably Roger," said Lydia apologetically. "He knows when Reggie's birthday is, and he must have guessed—"

Her mother laid a hand on her arm. "Tell him to call back, okay? We have so little time. . . ."

Lydia kissed her mother's cheek and went inside, giving Reggie's shoulder a little pat as she passed.

"Where have you been?" Angela called to Reggie. "Look who's here, your fellow fish, Eunice!" Angela turned to Eunice. "Reggie told me what a good time you had in the pool the other day. I hope you brought your suit tonight."

"I just came to deliver—"

"Are you gonna put my cakes in the refrigerator? Or are you trying to give us all food poisoning?"

Angela gave Eunice's head a pat. "Have you ever had champagne? Hurry back out so we can toast!"

In the kitchen Eunice just managed to squeeze the cakes into the packed refrigerator. Her arms had gone almost numb from holding the boxes so long. She turned to Reggie.

"Did you tell your mother I was coming to your party?" she demanded.

Reggie bent to examine her leg. "How do you like that? I already got a run. And these are Bill Blass panty hose my mother bought especially. They cost ten-fifty."

"I'm not coming to your party, Reggie."

"Who cares? I'm not either."

"You're really weird, you know that? You're World-Class Weird."

Reggie stuck out her tongue, which was the color of Hawaiian Punch. "Sticks and stones may break—"

"What's your problem anyway? Your mother's gone to all this trouble, your sister flew in from Boston, and you're still walking around with a two-ton chip on your shoulder. Do you like feeling sorry for yourself?"

Reggie reached for her ponytail. "Who do you think you are, talking to me like that? You've been hanging around with Joy McKenzie too much. You're getting as high-and-mighty as she is."

"You can just leave Joy out of this!"

"I saw her at her art class the other day, going around with her snotty chin in the air. Think she could even say hello to me?"

"She said you ran away before—"

"You'd run away, too, if somebody looked at you like you were a bug!"

The tile floor seemed to move a little under Eunice's feet. She lashed out at Reggie. "Always going around by yourself! What were you doing all alone, looking at dusty, boring old Oriental statues?"

"That shows how much you know. I like Buddhas! I like their smiles! And how do you know I don't like being by myself?"

"You don't even give people a chance to like you. You act so obnoxious—"

"Oh yeah? I'd rather be obnoxious than conceited, like her. I saw her leave you flat at the pool!"

"You've got a leak upstairs, Reggie! You've got a screw loose, you know that?"

"Oh yeah? Then how come she's not here with you? If you're such great partners? How come?"

"Reg, are you still pulling on that ponytail?" Lydia came into the kitchen and lifted her sister's hand from her hair. "You know you're going to cause brain damage."

It should have been a typical big-sister remark, but it wasn't. Lydia's tone totally lacked the essential antagonism. She might have been petting a runty puppy, telling it it was a dear little thing.

"What are you two doing in here anyway?" Lydia went on, moving toward the door. "It's your party!"

"Sure!" cried Reggie. "She didn't even buy any Hawaiian Punch!"

Lydia turned around, still wearing that there-there-it's-all-right smile. "Don't be a party pooper," she said coaxingly. "I know you've been looking forward to this, having Eunice here and everything. Mom told me."

"Mom's a big fat liar."

Lydia shook her head and pursed her lips. "Don't spoil everything for the rest of us, okay?" Without waiting for a reply, she hurried back outside, sliding the glass doors closed behind her.

Reggie watched her go with a face nearly purple with fury. "Go ahead. Run away from me! Treat me like one of your brain diseases!" she yelled at the closed doors.

Through the doors they could see her mother take Lydia by the arm and draw her close, and José at long last pop the champagne cork. As the champagne bubbled out, Angela and Lydia laughed and tried to catch it with their glasses.

"See!" cried Reggie. "They didn't even wait for me!"

"They've *been* waiting!"

"They could've waited a little longer!"

"For what? For you to come out and ruin everything?"

"I should've known! I should've known you'd be on their side, too, just like everyone else! Even my father! Even that phony, stupid counselor they tried to make me go to! I should've known!"

Reggie began to cry. She cried the way she did everything else, in the highest imaginable pitch, with great sputtering sobs, flinging herself into a chair and immediately catapulting herself out of it, spraying tears and, when she swiped at her veiny red nose, snot.

In the midst of it all she managed to hiccup out a few words, among which Eunice was able to understand "alone," "hate them all," and "care about themselves." Something in Eunice began to quiver, as if the waves of Reggie's grief had touched it.

"Reggie, come on. Stop! It's your birthday!"

"Go away. You don't know how I feel!"

"Yes, I do," Eunice heard herself say.

"Oh, sure!" Reggie gulped, then spun around and hissed, "Here she comes! Let's get out of here!"

She began running toward the stairs just as Angela slid open the glass doors.

"Regina Ackeroyd! Are you standing us up?"

"We're talking," Reggie flung back without stopping. "We're exchanging confidences, just the way you wanted us to. Come on, Eunice."

Angela, holding her slim champagne glass, looked at Eunice with a mixture of confusion and pleasure. "Are you?"

"Come on up here!" screamed Reggie.

Angela gave Eunice a little pat on the shoulder. "Don't let me interfere! I remember how important sharing secrets with a best friend is at your age! You two chat away. But promise you'll come down in time for the birthday cake, okay?"

"Right now!" shrieked the spider monkey.

Angela gave Eunice a farewell pat and a gentle push toward the stairs. As she hurried back outside she gave herself a small shake, as if shrugging off a burden she'd been carrying a long time.

"Get in here," said Reggie, apparently forgetting her dictum that only her closest friends were allowed to enter her room. The place was a filthy mess, dirty dishes, glasses with dried-up Hawaiian Punch in the bottom, comic books and magazines strewn everywhere. Reggie must not have hung up any clothes since 1980. On her bulletin board was a yellowed newspaper clipping of the graduation of her sister—two years younger than the rest of the class and the valedictorian—and a number of postcards of Oriental gardens and smiling Buddhas. On a table near her bed was a large Japanese doll covered by a glass dome thick with dust. Reggie stood in the middle of it all, her skin red and rashy, her nose dripping.

"Now you get the picture," she said. "My family hates me. They wouldn't care if I drowned in their stinking pool or got some horrible disease and died a painful death. They'd pretend to be sorry, so no one would guess what rotten hearts they have, but really they'd be glad."

Eunice removed some debris from a chair and slowly sat down. "Maybe you're right," she said quietly.

"What? What did you say?"

"Maybe they wouldn't care."

Reggie, whose arms had been spinning like windmills, grew abruptly still. "That's not what you're supposed to say."

"I told you I understand."

Reggie stared at her, then reached for a T-shirt hanging on the back of a chair and scrubbed at her nose. When she spoke, her voice was totally screechless. "I'll never fit in with them. If my mother and I didn't have the same bumps on our ears, I'd think I was adopted. Now I'm pretty sure I was just an accident."

"Where's your father?"

"They got divorced a long time ago. He's an engineer; he's in Japan this year. He was never home, and my mother hated having to hang around and take care of us all alone all the time. So after they split up, she decided she always wanted to be a doctor, and she started med school. That's how she is. I was just a baby. You know what that's like? Lyd and I were always with a baby-sitter. Lyd didn't care. The baby-sitters loved her; she was so cute and smart. I had allergies. I couldn't drink milk, and cats and grass made me break out in hives like volcanoes. Lyd decided she was going to be a doctor, too, and she used to stick Band-Aids all over me all the time, then pull them off. The baby-sitters thought that was so cute. Even Mrs. Sterling. You should've seen her fussing over Lydia this

78

afternoon. You think she ever fusses over me like that? Huh?"

Eunice didn't answer.

"When my mother was doing her internship and her residency, we didn't see her for whole days together. It used to seem like weeks to me. Sometimes she'd get an hour off and come home and wake me up in the middle of the night. She'd tell me how much she missed me. She'd even cry sometimes. Ha! I'd yell at her, 'Oh yeah? You can't trick me. I know you hate me! I know you hate to be with me!'"

"Her work's important. You told me so yourself."

"I knew you didn't understand! Of course, I know her work's important! I know she couldn't stay home and be a housewife. She's not the housewife type, anybody can see that. You think that kept me from missing her? At least I got over that. Now I don't care." Reggie threw the snotty T-shirt on the floor. "I'll never fit in with them. I'm not pretty, I'm not smart, and when I see blood, I feel like I'll keel over. They've both given up on me by now. Why do you think my mother keeps ordering cakes from you? And telling all her airhead friends about you? To bribe you, that's why. To get you to be my friend."

She must have an ulterior motive, Joy had insisted all along. Right, as always.

Losers. It took one to know one. There was still half the summer left, and now it seemed to stretch before Eunice like some endless desert road. In a few short days Eunice had become, like Reggie, a reject.

"That's not the only reason." Reggie nudged the disgusting T-shirt with her toe. Eunice looked up and saw that though Reggie's eyelids and nose were fiery red, the blotches had begun to fade from her arms and neck. She stood with her arms around herself, as if trying to keep her mercury blob of a self from splattering again.

"That's not the only reason she buys them. They're good cakes."

"Thank you."

Back outside Eunice sang "Happy Birthday" and thanked them

all for their lavish compliments on the cakes, but when Reggie, who was as obnoxious as ever toward her family, tried to catch her eye and smile at her, Eunice pretended not to see. And as soon as some of Lydia's friends dropped in, she took the excuse and left, though Angela pursued her all the way to her bike, trying to persuade her to stay and have a swim.

At home Eunice took pen and paper and locked herself in the bathroom. Leaning on the vanity among Millie's cleansers and astringents, she chewed her pen and ground her teeth. At last she wrote:

DEAR PHOEBE:
I never thought I'd have to write to you. But something so awful has happened, and there isn't anyone else I can talk to. Please help.

My best friend has left me flat. For a boy. This hurts me very much. But that's not even all. Another girl, who everyone in our class regards as a joke, if not worse, is trying to leech onto me. I do not want to go around with a reject, even now, when I feel more alone than I ever have in my whole entire life.

I don't know where to turn or what to do. Please send your reply in the enclosed self-addressed envelope ASAP. Thank you very much.

Yours very truly,
REJECT II

She didn't have to hesitate; she didn't have to cross out one word. The truth of her life spilled forth. Unwhitewashed Reality. "My best friend has left me flat."

"Eunice! Are you having trouble again?"

Eunice slipped the letter down the front of her T-shirt. When she opened the bathroom door, her mother laid a hand on her forehead.

"I think I'll make you an appointment with Dr. Wicks."

Eunice went up to her room. She put the letter under her pillow and fell asleep.

Fourteen

ALL NIGHT LONG she tossed and turned. No sooner did she fall asleep than she'd start awake, as if something sharp had poked her. She lay on her back, on her side, on her stomach, but the hard, pointy thing found her and jabbed her awake. She made her box springs squeak till Millie threatened to throw the clock radio at her if she didn't lie still.

At last, toward morning, Eunice sat up. As if she were, now, finally asleep and dreaming, she reached under her mattress. Her hand touched something hard, sharp, and pointy-edged. She drew out the red and white scrapbook. Without opening it, she held it on her lap for a long time. Then, like a sleepwalker, she carried it across the room and laid it in the very back of her closet.

All those years she'd slept with it, and never once had it bothered her. Eunice stumbled back to bed. She closed her eyes.

What seemed like moments later Russell was shaking her shoulder and waving a spatula in her face.

"Are you in a coma? Didn't you hear us calling? Joy's on the phone."

Eunice leaped up. "Joy?"

"And I made blueberry pancakes!" crowed Russell, as if all life's problems were suddenly, miraculously solved.

Eunice missed the bottom step and mashed her nose against the wall. She grabbed the phone as her mother said, "Your breakfast's on the table. Tell her you'll call back."

"Joy? Hello? Joy?"

"I just wanted to make sure you're coming to the pool with me this afternoon."

Eunice rubbed her eyes. She pulled the phone cord as far as it could go from the kitchen and into the living room. Had she dreamed yesterday? Was she dreaming now? How could Joy talk as if nothing had happened? A miracle *had* occurred.

That was it. Joy had come to her senses, realized Robert's magnificent head contained neurons plugged with peanut butter, and ditched him.

"You want me to come to the pool?"

"I'm meeting Robert at two-thirty. I'll come by your house a quarter after."

"How many times do I have to tell you? Don't stretch the cord like that!" called Mr. Gottlieb.

"And your pancakes are getting cold!" added Mrs. Gottlieb.

Eunice sat down on the couch. She hadn't dreamed. She wasn't dreaming now. There were no miracles, only Unwhitewashed Reality. Her mashed nose began to throb.

"Eu? Are you there?" Joy asked.

"More or less."

"Well? Can you be ready at two-fifteen?"

There on the couch lay the Sunday paper. Eunice turned to the living section and stared down at Dear Phoebe's photo. "I salute your dignity," read her first line of advice.

Even someone with a mashed nose and a pierogi body could have dignity.

"I'm not coming to the pool today."

"What do you mean?"

"I mean, I'm not coming."

"Why not?"

"You know why. I don't fit in."

"Fit in? Are you a puzzle piece or what?"

"I can't talk to those kids."

"You didn't even try, Eu! You expected them not to like you, so you didn't even try. If you'd just been yourself—"

"Tell Joy you have to come eat!"

"The way you sat there grinding your teeth like a cement mixer, it's no wonder they kept clear of you."

Mesmerized by Phoebe's perfect hair and unflinching gaze, Eunice understood. Joy's scheme was to foist Eunice off on the rest of the crowd, so she and Robert wouldn't have to bother with her. Then, Joy figured, she wouldn't have to feel she'd dumped her best friend. Well, she had another think coming.

"Let me give you some advice, Joy. You can't have your cake and eat it too."

"What?"

"Don't dish it out if you can't take it."

"Eunice . . ."

"Cool it, honey. Wake up and smell the coffee, dear."

"Are you possessed or what? Have you been sampling your father's peppermint schnapps again? What are you talking about?"

"If you want to choose Robert over . . . if you . . ."

"Eunice, listen to me. You know my motto. I live by it, right?"

"Sure. No sweat."

"I wouldn't be true to myself if I didn't tell you I'm interested in Robert Gray. I wanted to get to know him better. That doesn't mean you and I can't still—"

"I'm not coming to the pool with you. I have my dignity. I may not have a hot pink suit and a beautiful body," she put as much sneer into her voice as she could, "but I'm not a jerk either."

"You're jealous, Eunice Gottlieb."

Eunice gave a strangled yelp. "Now who's possessed? Jealous! You only wish I was jealous of you, Joy McKenzie! You only wish I wasn't telling you the plain, flat-out truth."

"Admit it. You'd love to have a boyfriend too."

"Ha! Double ha! Triple ha!"

"Are you coming to the pool with me or not?"

"I'd rather eat raw eel."

Joy's reply came without an instant's hesitation. "Fine. It's up to you."

"I know."

"Completely up to you."

"I'm glad you've finally realized that, Joy McKenzie."

"What are we anyway—Siamese twins?"

Eunice's eyes filled with tears. "Go ahead! Make our whole

friendship sound warped and weird! You're so smart! So good with words!"

"I hope you have an absolutely delightful day, sitting around sweating and feeling sorry for yourself. Good-bye."

Eunice slowly lowered the receiver and looked at it. She didn't have to add "sweating." She didn't have to go that far.

"Eunice, if I have to call you one more time . . ."

Eunice came into the kitchen and hung up the phone. Instantly it rang again.

"We'll have to have a board meeting to decide what this means for the business. Tomorrow afternoon, the office, one o'clock sharp." Click.

"Here's your pancakes, Eu-eu," said Russell. "I made blueberry today."

Eunice looked at her brother without seeing him, then ran upstairs and pulled on her clothes. She took two envelopes and, disguising her handwriting as best she could, addressed one to herself, the other to Dear Phoebe, c/o the newspaper.

Downstairs she rushed past her parents' questions and Russell's disappointment, out the door and to the corner mailbox.

She had done it. She had actually mailed Phoebe a letter. Leaning against the mailbox, she felt as if every day for years and years she'd walked past an orphanage and felt sorry for the little kids behind the fence only to wake up one morning and find herself in there with them. It was one thing to sympathize with other people's problems. It was a very different thing to admit that you, too, were so confused and alone you had to resort to writing to a complete stranger for help.

Maybe that was the strangest thing of all about truth: who it happened to.

She walked around for a while, unable to face her mother's "What's wrong?" or Russell's hopeful offer of a plateful of cold pancakes. The Yo-Yo Effect wouldn't work today. There was no reeling her back now. Her string was broken.

She walked and walked, though her legs had never felt so heavy. She remembered how she'd tossed and turned last night. When she pictured the red and white album, buried in the back of her closet among shoes that no longer fit and toys she'd broken or outgrown, she had to lean against a telephone pole for a while, she felt so bad.

Finally she was too tired to walk any farther. As she came in the door, Millie was just answering the phone and she held it out to Eunice.

"Make it quick, I have to call Richard."

"Hi," said Reggie. "Want to come in my pool?"

"Sorry, but I feel a little sick today."

After a tiny silence Reggie said, "From eating your own cake, probably. Ha-ha."

"Ha-ha. Probably."

"I'll call you tomorrow. Hope you feel better."

Feel better. The words held no meaning.

Millie snatched the receiver and dialed Richard's number. Their father, scowling over the sports page, said, "How many times do I have to tell you girls not to tie up the phone? What if someone's trying to reach us? What if there's an emergency?"

"Emergency—what is this, the White House or something?"

Her mother passed a hand over her eyes. "Eunice, Eunice, what's gotten into you? Sometimes I feel as if I hardly know you anymore."

Carrying the living section folded to "Dear Phoebe," Eunice went into the bathroom and locked the door. She gave each underarm a shot with Millie's deodorant, then looked at herself in the mirror. Why should her mother know her when she no longer knew herself? Her body was changing its shape and its smell without consulting her. She'd lost her best friend. And as she looked in the mirror she saw that her hair, which she must have forgotten to comb, had one hunk standing up at the crown. It looked, she thought with horror, as if she'd been yanking on it.

Fifteen

THE NEXT AFTERNOON Eunice folded up her Have Your Cake T-shirt, put it in her bike basket along with the few flyers she still had, and rode over to Joy's house. There was, of course, no way they could continue the business together. If she and Joy were going to divorce, Eunice wasn't getting involved in any nasty custody fight. Joy was entitled to the business since it had been her idea in the first place, and since she was the one who truly needed the income.

Through the screen door she could see Joy sitting at the kitchen table, wearing her bathing suit and cover-up, the business ledger open before her. Eunice knocked.

"Come in."

Eunice put the T-shirt and flyers on the table and sat down. Joy didn't look up.

"Meeting called to order. I have prepared a statement of our current assets." She passed a sheet of paper to Eunice. "My proposal is to sell you my share, making you and Ludmilla Gottlieb sole owners."

Eunice looked down at the sheet of figures, then across at Joy's bent head. So she did feel guilty after all. She was trying to make it all up to Eunice by giving her her share.

"Is my proposal seconded?"

"You don't have to do this. You're the one who needs the money, for your private lessons. Compared to you, I don't need—"

Joy finally met her eye.

"You don't second the proposal?"

"I can always get money for deodorant by baby-sitting. Or I can just go on sneaking Millie's."

Joy folded her arms before her. "This is a business meeting. How stockbrokers choose to spend their profits has nothing to do with the future of the company."

"I'm trying to tell you that you don't have to give me anything."

"Who said 'give'? I said 'sell.' " Joy lowered her head again and read from the sheet of figures. "As you can see, we are making a small but steadily growing profit. I'm sure you'll agree the business has great potential for growth. Once Thanksgiving and Christmas roll around there's no telling how much it could make. Therefore." She drew herself up. "I hope you'll agree seventy-five dollars isn't too much to ask for my share."

"Seventy-five dollars!" Eunice rose from her seat. "Seventy-five dollars!"

"It's a very reasonable price, if you take the long-range view."

"But—but seventy-five dollars won't buy you more than—what?—five or six private lessons."

Joy looked up, and Eunice saw that rare, telltale twitching of her cheek. "That's my problem," she said in a suddenly unsteady voice. "I told you this is a business meeting, not—"

"Joy! I want to know how you're going to pay for your private lessons."

"Let me worry about that, okay? I—I might not have time for them this year after all!"

"Not have time!" Eunice fell back in her chair. "For dance?"

"This is going to be a big year in school, a lot of extra work, and—"

Eunice stood up again. "That's not why! It's because you want to be with Robert Gray."

"Will you please stop jumping up and down? You're getting as hyper as Reggie Ackeroyd!"

"Admit he's destroying your brain! Talk about cretins!"

"You just can't help taking this whole thing personally, can you? You can't be businesslike! Here I am making you a lucrative offer, and all you can—"

"Okay, okay. You're absolutely right. To find a helping hand, you'd better look at the end of your own sleeve. Right. Why should I care if you're going to take the seventy-five dollars and blow it on miniskirts? Flimsy bathing suits instead of serious leotards? I second your proposal. Let's vote. All those in favor . . . aye."

"Aye. Motion carried. I'll give you the recipes file box, but obviously you'll have to find another kitchen."

"Don't worry about me."

"And you'd better call our regular customers and tell them the phone number's changed."

"I'll get new flyers out immediately."

"Good."

"Fine."

"That's it then. Meeting closed."

"Here." Joy handed Eunice the gray metal file box. "And good luck."

"There's no such thing as luck. It's all elbow grease." Eunice grabbed her T-shirt off the table. "I hope you don't mind if I pay you the seventy-five dollars in installments."

"Fine."

"Good."

"Excellent."

Eunice turned on her heel. But just as she opened the back door Joy said, "I want to say one thing. This is all your doing. I wanted to stay friends."

"Oh, sure! And pythons only want to give their victims sweet little hugs!" Eunice slammed the door, jumped onto her bike, and sped away.

What an idiot! she told herself as she pedaled along. *At least I don't have to feel so bad about her betraying me. She's even betraying dance for that peanut butter head. It's a positive blessing in disguise, finding out what a deceitful ninny I've been hanging around with all my life. She wants to stay friends! Ha! That's got to be the joke of the year! Of the century! As if the whole time we were sitting by that pool she wasn't secretly hoping I'd dive in and never come up again. As if she'd care if that truck coming toward me now ground me like graham cracker crumbs. As if . . .*

"Euuuuuuuuunice!"

A voice with all the appeal of screeching tires greeted her as she turned the corner into her street. Reggie came whizzing toward Eunice on her bike.

"I just happened to be in the neighborhood, so I thought I'd see if you felt better." Reggie skidded to a halt and peered at Eunice. "You look pretty yucky." She caught herself. "I mean, rotten."

"I never felt better in my life."

"Oh."

Eunice took the file box from her basket and dropped her bike on her front lawn. Reggie did likewise.

"My sister went back to Boston last night. Now my mother's trying to be real nice to me. She even came up in my room and tried to talk to me about how no matter how different children are mothers have places in their hearts for them all. 'Ha! Who do you think you're fooling?' I said. Then she told me to stop feeling sorry for myself all the time. She said I don't know how bad it makes her feel."

"And you said, 'Do you know how bad it makes me feel to be rejected by my own mother?' "

Reggie's eyes widened beneath their papery red lids. "I didn't think of that."

"Then you let her off too easy. You have to sock it to people, understand?" She marched across the lawn and into the house, Reggie at her heels. Sitting down at the kitchen table, she took the yellow legal pad her mother used to leave her instructions, flipped the page, and began to write. "IMPORTANT NOTICE TO OUR IMPORTANT CUSTOMERS!!!"

"What are you doing?"

"Quiet! I have to think!"

Reggie peered over her shoulder. "A new flyer for the business?"

"There are going to be some big changes around here."

Reggie yanked on her ponytail and did a little side-step. "You and Joy McKenzie had a fight, didn't you?" She could barely contain her glee. "Good for you! I always said she's the most conceited, uppity—"

"Cool it, honey."

IMPORTANT NOTICE TO OUR IMPORTANT
CUSTOMERS!!!

HAVE YOUR CAKE has changed its phone
number.

Now when you want to reach us to order our
delectable cheesecake, mousse, or Grandma
Gottlieb's famous strudel, just dial 555-5829.

But don't worry! Though we've changed our
number, our quality will stay the same!! Probably
better!!

So call today—and tell all your friends!!

Eunice read over what she'd written with satisfaction. But how
was she going to get it printed up? Her father worked in a plant
where he didn't have access to copying machines, and her mother,
being a Tempo worker, would never dare.

"You want me to help you ride around and put those in people's
mailboxes?"

"I have to get them made up first. Last time Joy's father did it.
Now I guess I'll have to go to a copy place and pay."

"My mother'll do it!" Reggie pranced across the floor. "Give it to me!"

Eunice watched Reggie collide with the refrigerator. Everything
about her—whether she was being offensive or attempting to win
you over—made Eunice wince, and yet . . . Eunice looked around
the kitchen, with her mother's ancient Mixmaster and the oven
that burned the left side of everything. Not to mention that her
mother would be constantly fretting about the mess she'd make—
and, come to think of it, the phone always ringing—Russell would
be poking his nose and probably his fingers into everything, Millie
would constantly be offering her invaluable, completely unsought
advice . . .

"She can just give it to a secretary. No problem! She'll love to do it!
She'll do handsprings!" Reggie tried to grab the paper. "Give it to me!"

Reggie's house was air-conditioned. The kitchen was supere-quipped, and Angela considered messiness the natural state of things.

"I'll give it to her right away!" yelled Reggie, lunging for the paper. "We'll have it by tomorrow morning!"

From a businesswoman's perspective there was no way she could throw away a valuable resource like Reggie. The fact that the more she considered the details of the business, the more doing it all alone frightened her—that fact had nothing to do with what she said next.

"Listen to me, Reggie. Stop hopping around for one minute, will you? There's a slight possibility we could work out a deal to make you a partner. Strictly business, understand?"

"Yeah, yeah, yeah," crowed Reggie, snatching the yellow sheet of paper off the pad.

"Strictly business!" Eunice hollered after her as Reggie went skittering out the door.

Sixteen

THE HEAT WAVE went on and on, so long that it became not a wave but an ocean of dust and dryness. The whole world smelled like hot tar. Gardens shriveled, air conditioners blew fuses, and Russell's crayons melted all over the front steps. The Indians had a record losing streak going, and who could blame them? It was impossible to imagine getting up the energy to lift a spoon, let alone swing a bat. Millie slumped home from Burger King every day, whimpering about how tired she was. "Even my ears are tired," she'd murmur, dragging off her earrings. She and Richard spent all their free time at the ninety-nine-cent movies, watching *Revenge of the Nerds* till Millie muttered lines from it in her sleep.

Mrs. Gottlieb just surrendered. On days she didn't have to go to work she sat out in the backyard with her feet in the old baby pool, reading magazines. The kitchen floor got dirty, and the end tables dusty, and she didn't even care. It was eerie. Having her bare feet stick to the kitchen floor made Eunice feel as if she were in the wrong house. But that wasn't the only unnatural thing about those weeks.

Every day Eunice rode her bike to Reggie's. The streets she pedaled on were hushed and empty. With the heat blasting her from all sides Eunice felt as if the world had become one mammoth kiln and she and the houses and trees she passed were being baked into petrified stillness. The life seemed to have gone out of everything.

Then she'd see Reggie in the front doorway, all aquiver, her ponytail waving back and forth. She was, it seemed, the one breathing being in the entire parched, deserted landscape. Eunice would drop her bike and step into that oasis of central air-conditioning. The coolness would wash over her, and her body would slowly begin to revive.

Not her mind, though. Answering the phone with "Have Your Cake!," using Angela's Cuisinart and convection oven, carrying on the business with Reggie hopping around dropping things and Mrs. Sterling standing in the doorway silently, wringing her hands over what they were doing to her kitchen, were all too strange and wrong, like seeing her mother relaxing. Eunice's brain kept resisting.

You are not really here with Reggie the Reject. Repeat. You are not really here.

"Cream cheese."
"Cream cheese."
"Sugar."
"Sugar."
"Eggs."
"Eg—oops."

Every day Eunice told herself that this period of her life was only temporary. It was just a matter of time before Joy got sick of sitting beside that pool, her brain turning to peanut butter and her hamstrings to jelly. Only a matter of time, Eunice told herself, her teeth setting, before Joy comes back, and everything is just the way it used to be.

But when would that be? She could just see Joy, so absorbed in Robert Gray she'd forget to put on her sunscreen. She'd sit there getting skin cancer, all for him. What if *he* offered to put the sunscreen on her? She'd tilt her chin and reply, "Egad! Absolutely not!" Wouldn't she? His eyes were so black. Joy could probably see herself in them. He'd buy her a can of pop and she'd drink it, though she never drank pop, just because *he'd* bought it for her. What would that be like, to have a boy buy you pop? To have him watch you drink it, then take a sip from the same can? To pass it back and forth, fingers touching? What would that be like, to wake up in the morning and remember, first thing, that there was a boy waking up and thinking of *you*, first thing? Even if he was a boy with a geranium in his cranium?

The jerk!

Every day Eunice rushed home from Reggie's and searched through the mail. But Dear Phoebe's reply was never there.

All during the endless, steamy afternoons Reggie and Eunice sat in Reggie's kitchen, waiting for the phone to ring. Together they watched the minute hand sweep around the face of Angela's numberless kitchen clock. Eunice often urged Reggie to go have a swim, but Reggie seemed to prefer sitting beside Eunice to any other place in creation.

One particularly slow day Eunice idly took out one of her word-finder puzzle books. Reggie immediately ran upstairs and came back with a crossword puzzle book. As Eunice searched for the hidden word *detergent*, Reggie inked in her squares with such rapidity Eunice knew once and for all she was nuts. Scribbling away like that! And in ink! But when she looked over Reggie's shoulder she saw her write "Katmandu."

"Katmandu?"

"The capital of Nepal."

"The capital of Nepal?"

"It's a real common one. Like Circe, you know, the lady who turned men into pigs?"

Eunice saw that the squares were inked in with real words. "You're a pro at this, aren't you?"

Who'd ever have suspected that a girl who used "yucky" in every other sentence had a vocabulary that included Katmandu? Not that a person could work "Katmandu" into her everyday conversation. Still, it was impressive.

Reggie laid down her pen and reached for her ponytail. "It's strange. I can do these puzzles with my eyes closed, but I always flunk vocabulary tests. My brain just gets all lumpy, like sour milk. That counselor they sent me to said I expect to fail, so I do."

Eunice seemed to have heard the same thing somewhere. "Do you think that's true?"

94

Reggie shrugged again, and gave her ponytail a workout. "How should I know? All I know is a lot of stuff I can do fine when I'm alone I mess up when I'm with other people. It's like I'm—what do they call it?—a split personality. When I can't go to sleep at night, you know what I think about?" She leaned toward Eunice, clasping her hands between her knife blade knees. "I think about going to Japan and becoming a Buddhist monk. They don't even have to talk to each other. They just work in their garden and look at the moon and meditate. You couldn't mess that up."

And she tugged on her plume so hard Eunice had to look away to keep from grabbing her hand and begging her to stop it.

Seventeen

THOUGH AT FIRST Reggie sent expenses skyrocketing, smashing eggs and knocking over cups full of cream, she remembered everything Eunice told her, and after a week she began to relax enough to clean up her mistakes without making a worse mess. She didn't mind doing the worst jobs, like scrubbing out the pots coated with chocolate or crushing graham cracker crumbs with a rolling pin.

"Look," Reggie said the first time they went to the supermarket together. "There's graham crackers already ground up."

"They're more expensive," said Eunice, echoing Joy's argument against them.

"Yeah, but the time we spend grinding them up, you know. Not that I mind or anything! But maybe if you figure it out, the time we spend crushing them instead of doing other stuff, maybe they're worth it." She looked at Eunice timidly. "You know?"

Eunice looked at the box of crumbs and realized she was terrified of doing anything differently from the way Joy had. Why was that? She'd bought Joy out; she didn't have any obligation to her. But taking Reggie's advice over Joy's was turning the world upside down.

"No," she told Reggie firmly. "Put them back."

When they'd finished the morning's baking, Reggie made them lunch. Every day it was the same thing: tomato sandwiches and Hawaiian Punch. Reggie sliced the tomatoes thick and gobbed on so much Miracle Whip the sandwiches fell apart the instant they were picked up. They were soggy, disgusting, and delicious. Reggie ate three or four, washing them down with tankards of punch. For dessert there were always Devil Dogs, Sno Balls, or Twinkies.

"Don't ever eat those things in public, understand?" Eunice instructed her. "No gourmet would be caught within ten feet of a Sno Ball. You have a reputation to uphold."

Reggie crammed the rest of the Sno Ball into her mouth and wriggled in her chair. Gulping down the cake, she said ecstatically, "I know, partner!"

Every morning, when Eunice left her own house, she told herself she would absolutely not spend one minute more than necessary with Reggie. But every day, when call-in hours ended, she couldn't resist. Upstairs, in Reggie's travesty of a room, she slipped into Lydia's jade green suit. Reggie invariably raced ahead, cannonballing into the water and thrashing her way to the side. Eunice slipped in from the side, and the water world folded her in its cool arms. Every day it welcomed her, soothed her, told her how strong she was. The clay crust the day had baked around her cracked and fell away.

Then she'd lift her head and see Reggie on the edge of the pool, leaning forward to watch, her teeth chattering and eyes popping.

"You're a good swimmer," she told Eunice.

"How come you're not, with a pool like this? It's a miracle you haven't drowned by now."

Reggie's face fell. She reached for her ponytail. Eunice, so serene a moment before, felt her teeth set.

"I'm only saying it for your own good. What if you fell out of a boat or something?"

"You sound just like my mother," said Reggie, feebly. "She made me take swimming lessons. Diving lessons too. She hired a private teacher and everything."

"So how come you didn't learn?"

"I'm not learning something just 'cause she wants me to! Besides, I couldn't. The teacher made me too nervous. Anyway, my mother doesn't really care!" Her voice was reaching for its old whine. "She'd just as soon see me drowned anyway! She's just like Joy. All she cares about is herself. All she cares—"

"Do you have to blame everything on your mother?"

Now Reggie truly looked betrayed. "I thought . . . You said—"

"Just forget your mother for once," snapped Eunice. "Do it for yourself, that's what I'm trying to tell you. Show a little independence. You'll feel better. No one likes a leech, you know. No one likes a wimp who can't stand on her own two feet."

"You should talk," muttered Reggie. "You won't even try graham cracker crumbs."

"What did you say?"

"Never mind."

When Eunice got home, her mother told her that she'd just gotten a two-week job and Eunice would be in charge of babysitting Russell while she was gone. Russell raised his head from his Play-Doh to smile benignly at his big sister.

"What the h-e-c-k . . ."

"Eunice Enid Gottlieb!"

"What the heck are you doing always messing around with that Play-Doh?"

"I'm making the world," replied Russell.

"Oh yeah? Didn't God do it good enough for you the first time?"

Mrs. Gottlieb passed a hand over her eyes.

"Not the whole world, really," Russell explained. "Just North and South America, Europe, and Africa. I want to see for myself if they fit together."

"What for? It's already proved. It was right in *National Geographic*. Once everything was whole, and now everything's in separate pieces."

"I just want to see for myself," Russell repeated patiently. "It's so hard to believe, that things could change so much." He gently shaped a little ridge with two fingers. "Do you think they'll ever get back together again?"

Eighteen

TWO DAYS LATER Eunice had to do an emergency heavy cream run to Stop 'n' Shop. She had Russell in tow, and though they had a rush job, he was dawdling in the frozen foods aisle, leaning over one case after another to feel the cold air on his face.

"Wow, look at this!" he was saying. "Frozen popcorn! I didn't know they had frozen popcorn!"

"Of course they have frozen popcorn; they have frozen everything. Now come on."

Russell considered this. "Not eggs," he said. "They don't have frozen eggs!" He began to go into one of his usual ecstasies over one of his usual kooky discoveries, his round cheeks getting pink and his eyes bigger than ever.

"All right, Russell," said Eunice, laughing in spite of herself. "Give me a break!"

"But it's important! You shouldn't say 'everything' because there's always something that's not everything. Stuff's changing every minute, you know? Even when you're saying 'now,' it's already 'then.' Just think of that."

Eunice was suddenly covered with goose bumps, and they weren't from Russell's philosophical revelations or from standing around the Popsicles so long. She'd just caught a glimpse of very familiar hamstrings, flashing out from under a hot pink romper. She considered diving into the peas frozen in butter sauce, but at the end of the aisle Joy zoomed on by, pushing a cart, with Robert Gray in her wake.

"The whole world's changing right while we stand here! Stars are exploding! The continents are drifting!" cried Russell, so that a woman passing by looked at Eunice as if to say, *Poor child! Is he taking anything for it?* Eunice ran up the aisle and, concealing herself behind a mountain of mayonnaise, spied on Joy.

They were nearly to the other end of the aisle, and Eunice couldn't see Joy's face clearly, but she thought the dreamy, half-awake look was gone from it. Robert held up a bag of barbecued chips for her inspection. She brushed it aside and reached for a box of melba toast. Robert Gray looked at it as if it were ten-day-old hamburger.

"What are you doing? What are you looking at?"

"Ssshh!" Eunice shoved Russell back around the mayonnaise display. Of course she'd known Joy and Robert were spending all their time together. Of course she'd known Joy had gone on living without her. But somehow she hadn't really known it until now.

"Guess what I just thought of? Frozen peanut butter. Great, huh? You and Reggie could sell it!"

Joy would never have ducked behind the mayonnaise or dived into the peas. Joy would have sailed straight on down the aisle toward Eunice and Russell, her chin in the air, even if their situations had been reversed and she were the one in a wrinkled sundress with her grubby little brother and Eunice were the glowing, beautiful one with a boyfriend. Joy was going full speed ahead with her life and Eunice, her goose bumps burgeoning, realized she was too. Here she was, shopping. She'd go over to Reggie's and bake; she'd deliver; she'd make money. The customers were satisfied, and the business was going along just as smoothly and profitably as ever, without Joy.

I'm here and she's there, and we're both still alive. Eunice shivered, letting herself into something.

"We could stick little marshmallows in it. I bet people'd buy it. You and Reggie could add it to your line."

Joy let Robert drop the barbecued chips into the cart. Then she nestled her own melba toast in carefully and was off again, with Robert trying to keep up. Eunice stared at the spot, way down at the other end of the aisle, where they'd been.

"Can we buy some peanut butter? And marshmallows?"

"Go look if Joy's in the checkout line. And if she is, don't let her see you, understand?"

Russell raced back to report he'd just seen Joy leave, holding hands with a boy.

"How come her hair's green? Can we buy the peanut butter? Huh?"

"Okay. And maybe one other thing . . ."

"What?" screeched Reggie when Eunice unpacked the groceries on her kitchen table. "Graham cracker crumbs! But you said—"

"Never mind what I said, Reggie, okay? Let's just get these cakes done so we can go swimming."

"Maybe you'll try the new route I worked out too."

"What?"

"Well, I got to thinking." Reggie began to reach for her ponytail but instead crammed her hand into her shorts pocket. For the first time since Eunice had known her, Reggie's hair wasn't yanked into its usual plume. It still stood up, more or less, so used to standing on end it didn't know how to relax and lie down. But a few hairs curled around Reggie's face, softening its peakedness. "You know how you and Joy always delivered to the most important customers first? That doesn't make sense. There's more direct routes. And in this heat I think we ought to deliver stuff the quickest way possible."

"But we always—" Eunice didn't know if she stopped herself or if Reggie interrupted.

"I got it all worked out. Just look." And she unfolded a wad of Hawaiian Punch-stained paper, on which she'd drawn a map of all the streets where they delivered. "You are here," she said, pointing. "Now look. If we—"

Eunice could see at a glance that Reggie had figured it all out with the quick, sure intelligence she could call up only when she was by herself.

"What do you think?"

"I can see it's a lot more logical."

Reggie threw her arms around herself and beamed.

That night, after they had made the deliveries using the new route, and after she'd congratulated Reggie on its efficiency and said good night, Eunice put ten dollars into an envelope. On a piece of paper she wrote:

Sum due	$75.00
Minus	$10.00
Still owe	$65.00

Yours truly,

EUNICE E. GOTTLIEB

She put the paper in with the money and addresssed the envelope:

Ms. Joy McKenzie
PERSONAL URGENT CONFIDENTIAL

Doing her Houdini act, she slipped out the front door and rode to Joy's. Joy's old joke had been: "I don't have to steer my bike, I just give it its head, and it goes straight to the Gottliebs' ."

The lights were on in the living room. Eunice dropped her bike on the front lawn and went around to the back door, as always. She had to knock twice before Mrs. McKenzie came.

"Eunice! We haven't seen you in so long! I'm sorry, but Joy's not here. She went to a party. Would you like a glass of lemonade?"

She'd told herself Joy might be out. Yet Eunice wasn't ready for the sharp little pain just under her heart. A party. Eunice had never been invited to a boy-girl party, but a hazy picture formed in her brain: a room with dark corners, girls in new clothes, laughing, whispering together. Boys watching them, darting out and asking them to dance. All the best music playing, and the air shimmering with the same rosy light Joy's suit cast.

"Eu-eu? A nice cold glass of lemonade?"

"Huh? Oh, no, no thanks. I—could you just give her this, please?"

Mrs. McKenzie took the envelope. "Her father's going to pick her up in forty-five minutes or so. Would you like to ride along?"

Didn't grown-ups know anything?

"That's okay. Just give her that envelope, please."

Mrs. McKenzie asked her in again for lemonade, then said good night. Eunice went down the back steps. Joy's pink bathing suit was on the line, along with her snowy white towel.

Did she get a new dress for the party? Did she fix her hair a way I never saw it before? For her recitals she always needed me to help her. I was the one who had to make sure her hair was just right and wouldn't come loose.

In the hot, still night the bathing suit and towel hung motionless.

Eunice rode home slowly. She rarely rode after dark. Moving through the heavy night air was somehow like swimming and made her feel a little calmer. At home there was a message by the phone: "Reggie A. called. She used her mother's computer to figure out the graham cracker crumbs will definitely be cost-effective (?????)"

"When God closes a door," Dear Phoebe wrote to Grieving in North Carolina, "He always opens a window."

Eunice was too tired to try to figure out what that meant. Without taking off her clothes, she threw herself on her bed and fell asleep.

Nineteen

THE HEAT WAVE and the Indians' losing streak broke on the same day.

And something else.

Eunice, Reggie, and Russell were in the Ackeroyds' kitchen, getting ready for the day's baking. Russell sat at the table, alternately poking marshmallows into peanut butter and his mouth. Reggie was measuring graham cracker crumbs, and Eunice was puréeing blueberries. They all were working so intently it was awhile before they realized how dark the room had grown.

"Wow," said Reggie, going to the sliding glass doors. "Is it the end of the world or what?"

Eunice came to stand beside her. A wild wind had blown up. It whipped through the trees, making the branches stream straight out. As she and Reggie stood there, it hurled itself against the house, rattling the heavy plate glass doors. The sky was the same pale, unearthly green as the leaves spun inside out in the wind.

"Better turn on the radio," said Russell, "and see if it's a tornado watch."

He began swinging the dial around. At the sound of a man's voice yelling they all stood still. But it was only a sports announcer, going berserk because Hargrove had just hit a grand-slam homer.

Two enormous peals of thunder sent Russell diving for Eunice's knees, and then it began to rain with such force that it sounded like rocks pounding down on the metal patio furniture. As Eunice and Reggie ran around closing windows, the air that hit their faces was suddenly fresh and cool. Eunice threw up a screen and leaned out.

"Hey!" yelled Reggie, pulling her back. "Get in here! It's lightninging. I don't want a charcoal-broiled friend!"

"Oh, Reg, it feels so goooood! It feels so cold! It tastes like ferns!" Eunice was pulling off her sandals.

"How do you know what ferns taste like? What are you doing?"

"Going out in it, of course!"

"You can't! You'll get all wet!"

"I always said you were a genius, Reg!"

"You'll get struck by lightning! You'll get pneumonia! You'll—"

"Don't be a wimp!"

Outside, the whole world was water, and Eunice melted straight into it. She was soaked to the skin in an instant. Rain ran down her cheeks, her arms, her legs; rain squished up between her toes. It beat on her head and on the metal lawn table, with a drum-drum-drumming that set her dancing. She whirled around. She flung her arms out. She took a flying leap and slid across the slick grass. She ran and stood beneath the gushing gutter, letting the rain pour over her. As if the rain were washing away some old, used-up Eunice, she felt giddy and new. She felt like a plant just sprung through the earth.

"I can't see! I'm drownding!"

Reggie came stumbling across the lawn, her eyes squeezed shut and her arms stretched straight out in front of her like a sleep-walker. Eunice ran and grabbed her hands. Holding tight, she leaned back and spun Reggie around and around. Reggie howled, but Eunice didn't let go, and then she felt Reggie lean back too. Their heels digging into the wet lawn, mud flying up, they spun each other as hard and as fast as they could, till they were no longer two people but one crazy spinning top that might any moment take off and spiral clean out of sight

"Eunice!"

"Reggie!"

Somehow their feet got tangled, and they collapsed on the grass.

"Are you okay?"

"No! I'm dying! I'm sick! I'm going to be dizzy for the rest of my life!"

"Let's do it again!"

"Okay!"

But Russell, in a voice that seemed to hail from across the ocean, was calling out the back door.

"There's a phone call! For a cake! Hurry up!"

Eunice sprang across the grass. She felt so light and buoyant that it was like swimming with both feet on the ground.

"Have Your Cake!"

"Is this the caterer?"

"At your service, ma'am!"

"I saw your ad in the paper."

"I'm so glad!"

Now Reggie came staggering through the glass doors. She looked so horrendous, half drowned and splattered with mud, and had such a goofy grin on her face, Eunice had to clap a hand over her mouth to keep from shouting out a laugh.

"I'm Mrs. Gray. My son's having a party."

Reggie took a corner of her shorts and squeezed out half a lake. Russell came running down with two big towels, but Eunice shook her head at him. Outside, the rain had begun to let up, and nothing had ever felt better than that breeze wafting across her wet new skin.

"His name's Bobby. Maybe you know him."

"Bobby?"

Reggie was wringing out the tails of her shirt now. All of a sudden she quacked. Eunice choked, trying not to laugh. "I don't think so!"

"He goes to the junior high? Anyway, one of his friends is moving away, and somehow I got talked into having a going-away party here. That kid can talk me into anything. Do you do things like going-away cakes?"

"Of course!" At the moment Eunice would have agreed to bake a wedding cake for four hundred people. She could do anything, and then some.

Then Reggie tapped Eunice on the shoulder and hissed, "Who is it?" in her ear. Eunice shrugged and mouthed the words *Mrs. Gray*. Reggie stepped back, her face taking on a funny look, as if she were about to get dizzy all over again.

"It's for this Saturday. Pretty short notice, I know."

"No problem, Mrs. Gray." Eunice watched Reggie back farther away and sit down. Something began to tap at the back of her own brain. Bobby . . .

"Great. Now I just want a plain cake, but there has to be plenty of it, the way these kids eat. . . ."

As Eunice worked out the details of it with her, Reggie sat staring out the window, her wet hair sticking to her cheeks like orange spaghetti.

At last Mrs. Gray, who was especially anxious about the price, seemed satisfied. Eunice repeated her order.

"That's for this Saturday, six o'clock."

"Right. The party starts at seven. Now just give me that price again?"

Eunice put the receiver down. Very slowly, as if underwater, Reggie turned to stare at her.

"*The* Mrs. Gray?" She spoke so quietly, letting each word fall with such deliberateness, that if Eunice weren't looking at her, she'd never have believed it was Reggie talking. Eunice began to realize how chilled she was.

"What—what do you mean, *the*—"

"You know what I mean."

"No . . ."

"It's Robert Gray's mother, isn't it? Isn't it?"

"He's having a party. She talked so fast!"

There was a moment when the only sound was a roll of distant thunder, and then Reggie jumped up. "And you said yes? You didn't tell her to go jump in the lake? Take a walk off the top of the Terminal Tower? You said you'd bake a cake for that walking rat vomit?"

"I don't know. I couldn't think. I was feeling so happy I didn't—" Eunice, freezing now, grabbed the towel from Russell.

"I can't believe it. I can't believe you said we'd slave over a hot stove and bake a cake, not just any cake but one of our wonderful, fantastic cakes, for *them*. After what they did to you. The way they treated you. You know she'll be there! You can carry humiliation just so far, you know! And then something has to snap!"

Eunice pulled the towel tighter around herself, but it didn't help. She saw that she was standing in a big puddle and thought she'd probably get pneumonia. Maybe she'd get really, really sick, and have to be hospitalized, and everyone would have to take care of her and feel sorry for her. Then all this nightmare, upside-down world would . . .

"You might as well stop grinding your teeth," Reggie said. "That's not going to help anything, and you look like a grizzly bear."

"Don't talk to me like that, Reggie Ackeroyd." Eunice heard her faint voice, as if she were already on her deathbed.

"Why not? You talk to me exactly like that. And look at this mess you've gotten us into. I have a right to be ticked off."

Where had Reggie learned to stand up for herself like that? Eunice leaned against the counter. Russell rushed to the stove.

"I'll make some tea," he said.

"Business is business," Eunice said in that same weak voice. "I couldn't turn down an order just because—"

"Egad!" shrieked Reggie. "Of course you could! It's your business! It's your life! Don't be such a wimp!"

Russell was hovering over the kettle, urging it to boil. Eunice thought—if what she was capable of just then could be called thought—how wonderful it would feel to surrender to Reggie's ire. To let Reggie sweep her along in her rage and righteous revenge. Just to keep Reggie going, she said, "We have to bake the cake. I said we would."

"Oh, we'll bake it all right! As soon as the rain stops, I'll go to the hardware store. Ant traps, D-Con, a little ground-up glass in the buttercream—oh, we'll bake them a cake all right!"

Eunice took the tea from Russell. He was staring at her with wide brown eyes. His sister, a homicidal maniac.

"We can't do that," Eunice said, spurring Reggie on. "We'd get caught for sure, and arrested, and—"

"There are times in life when you can't think about consequences! There's such a thing as justice, you know." Reggie was ablaze in a way Eunice had never before seen. The mosquito had metamorphosed into a fierce mother lion protecting her cub.

Just let her take over, make all the decisions, tell me how I should feel and what I should do . . .

Just the way Joy used to.

"Life is no egg," Eunice heard herself say. "You can always pick up the pieces."

Reggie stopped in her tracks. "What?"

"It's just something I read somewhere."

Reggie gave her a look, then started up again. "Okay, maybe we shouldn't poison them to death. But we can refuse to make the cake. If you won't call up, I will."

"You'll stutter."

"I will not."

"You'll break out in hives."

"I don't care."

"Reg, we have to make it. And not with any roach powder or anything."

Russell heaved a tremendous sigh of relief. "Drink your tea, Eu," he said in a grateful voice.

Reggie, her arms akimbo, glared at them both. "So she's still got you under her spell, huh? Even long distance she can get you to do whatever she wants. A puppet, that's all you are!"

"No, I'm not! And the only way I can prove it is to make that cake. Don't you see, Reg? If we refuse, we're saying Robert Gray and—and Joy have power over us. We're saying we'll pass up a profit because of them. But if we make it, if we go ahead with business as usual, it's saying we're free of them. They're just like any other people."

Reggie reached for the ponytail that wasn't there anymore, then crammed her fists into the pockets of her soaking shorts. After a while she said, "That makes sense, but it makes me feel rotten. I want to sock it to them."

"Here," said Russell, "have some tea. You're both all blue."

"Then you'll help me make the cake?" Eunice asked.

Reggie kicked a chair leg. "We're partners, aren't we?"

"Go on up and change your clothes," said Russell. "Get into something warm."

On the way up to her room Reggie said, "I probably wouldn't have been able to go through with it. Rat poison, I mean. But you know what? That's the maddest I've ever been in my life. Madder than at my mother or my sister or our whole class. I guess, I mean, I sure don't like to see you get messed over, I guess that's why."

Eunice, a few steps ahead, didn't turn around. But after she'd put on a pair of Reggie's designer shorts, which she couldn't zip, and a T-shirt that read JUST WHAT THE DOCTOR ORDERED she said, "Thanks for saying that, Reg. It means a lot."

When she and Russell got home, their father was pouring himself a beer, though he never drank beer except on Saturday nights.

"Those Indians—it's a miracle! If the rain had come ten minutes sooner, they'd have called it for sure! When the Yanks came to bat, it poured. Too late—it was already a complete game!"

Mrs. Gottlieb put down the potato she was peeling. "Give me a sip. I'm reborn. Feel that air!" She took a sip of the beer and smiled up at her husband. "So your poor old losers came through for once."

But Mr. Gottlieb shook his head. "I keep telling you, Doris. There are losers, and there are underdogs. And they're not the same at all."

Twenty

REGGIE AND EUNICE baked Robert Gray's cake early in the morning. Reggie worked in grim silence. At one point, when Eunice called for the baking powder, Reggie passed her a can of Ajax, but one look from Eunice and she put it back.

They made a cake for a baby shower order too.

The cakes were in the oven and they were loading the dishwasher when Reggie's mother, dressed in a crisp white summer robe, swept into the kitchen. She stretched both arms over her head and gave her tousled head a vigorous shake.

"Yum-yum! This wonderful fresh air! This wonderful sweet smell! My two favorite caterers in the world!" She kissed them both soundly on the foreheads, and Eunice noticed that Reggie's ducking away was only halfhearted. "You wouldn't let me snitch a slice of one of those cakes for breakfast, would you? You know, as a sideline, you should bottle that glorious smell and sell it. People would buy it up by the case!"

Reggie gave a loud belch and continued jamming bowls and spoons into the dishwasher. Her mother patted her head.

"Isn't Reggie's hair lovely, Eunice? I'm so glad she's given up that ponytail. I'm trying to get her to go down to Lucette's and get it really styled, but she says no." Angela reached for a coffee mug. "Maybe you could talk her into it. You certainly have more influence than I do."

"Nobody can make me do anything." But there was a new mildness to Reggie's growl, almost as if she were playing a part in a play and her heart weren't completely in it anymore. "I do what I want to do, and that's it."

"Those words are music to my ears," said Angela, patting her daughter's head again. Reggie pulled away, but Angela grabbed her elbow and said quickly, "You know that's all I want. For you to be happy."

This time Reggie's belch approached breaking the sound barrier. Angela, beaming away, poured herself some coffee from the computerized pot. "Doesn't it just beat everything how this business of yours has taken off? But what are you going to do when school starts? Do you realize that's less than a month away? You'll never be able to keep this up."

"We're dropping out," said Reggie, slamming the dishwasher door.

"We haven't really thought about that yet," said Eunice. Through the glass of the convection oven she watched Robert Gray's cake turning golden.

"Maybe you could make it just a summer thing," Angela said.

"No way!" yelled Reggie. "This is a serious business. This partnership's a lot more important than stupid, disgusting school, right, Eu?"

School. As she floated in Reggie's pool that afternoon the approach of school loomed before Eunice like her own tombstone. It wasn't just the usual sinking August feeling of knowing she'd have to exchange doing whatever she pleased for getting up in the dark, trudging through snow and ice to hear about how the trilobites died out and how to compute the area of a trapezoid, to do jumping jacks and to chew the cafeteria's cardboard pizza, and then trudging back home and doing homework till her brain curdled. Not to mention having to put up with burned-out teachers, Amazon bullies, and the people who could make you feel everything about you was wrong when a moment before, you'd felt just right.

School was not Eunice's favorite place on earth. But it had never been too bad, because Joy was there.

Now Joy wouldn't be there. Not for Eunice.

Now she would have Reggie at her heels. Reggie the Reject, at this very moment gasping for air at the other end of the pool. People would lump them together. When people saw her with Reggie, she'd automatically become a reject too.

I could drown her. It'd be easy enough to make it look like an accident.

Reggie came paddling toward her. Was her stroke a little stronger, or was Eunice just imagining it? How strange, the way people got to know each other. It was like that wooden folk doll that opened to show another smaller doll inside, then another and another. Only with people did it ever end? Could you ever finally say, "Here it is, the center nugget, right in my hand"? Could you pin a real live person down like that?

As she watched Reggie swim toward her, it was hard for Eunice to remember that the only reason she'd ever been nice to her was to get her hands on her Cuisinart. Two months before, it would have been as hard for her to believe she could like Reggie as it was to believe a gorilla and a kitten could fall in love.

Reggie came up for air, spouting like a whale. "Want to eat here? My mom said she'll cook out if we want."

"Thanks, but I'd better go home."

"Okay. Are you absolutely, positively sure you don't want me to sprinkle on a touch of Roach Prufe?"

Twenty-one

AT FIVE-THIRTY, wearing her Have Your Cake T-shirt and a brand-new pair of jeans and with her armpits drenched in the deodorant she'd finally bought herself, Eunice wheeled up in front of the Ackeroyds'. Reggie sat on the steps waiting. As they boxed the cakes—a cheesecake with a little stork perched in the corner, the sheet cake with "GOODBYE AND GOOD LUCK GARY written across it (Reggie had practiced over and over again on cookie sheets)—Eunice felt electrical currents running all through her, making her arms and legs prickle, her heart pound, and her stomach spin like the wheel in a hamster's cage.

"Ready?" asked Reggie.

"As I'll ever be."

Reggie reached across her handlebars and squeezed Eunice's hand. She had fixed her hair a new way, pulling it back from her face and fastening it with big clips that said "REGINA." It looked awful. Her bony forehead stuck out all the more, and so did her pointy little ears, one with a bump just like her mother's. She, too, wore her best jeans and had put new Day-Glo laces in her sneakers.

They dropped off the shower cake first, and as they turned their bikes toward Robert Gray's, the electrical currents juiced up so that Eunice could barely pay attention to where she was going.

"Look out!" yelped Reggie, but it was too late. Eunice rode right over a beer bottle smashed on the side of the road. Her front tire was slashed. They stared at it, then at each other.

"Now what are we going to do?"

"You'll have to ride over by yourself," Eunice said. "I'll walk my bike home."

Reggie turned pale. "By myself? I never made a delivery by myself before! I'll panic! I'll throw up!"

"All right then, give me your bike and I'll do it myself."

"What if Robert answers the door? Or her? You're gonna face them alone?"

"They're—they're just people. They fart like everyone else." Eunice reached for Reggie's bike but tripped and would have sent the cake smashing onto the street if Reggie hadn't grabbed the handlebars in time.

"You're in no condition to ride all the way alone. You're a nervous wreck. Half a block, and you and the cake will both be in smithereens. We'll walk."

"It's at least half a mile! We'll be late!"

Reggie already had the cake in her arms. "Then we'll be late. Now lock up the bikes and let's get going."

They took turns carrying the big white box. How could a "light golden cake" feel so heavy? They marched along without speaking. It was a perfect summer evening—crickets; fireflies; a gentle breeze tickling their ears and offering little bouquets of scent to their noses. The heat wave had broken just in time for Robert Gray's party. The commotion inside Eunice roared louder and spun faster as she marched toward these people even the weather bowed to.

"Here's the street. Number forty-nine."

They could hear music blaring in the backyard. It surrounded them, filling the night, as they stood there on the sidewalk.

"The party's already started," whispered Eunice, her throat so dry she could barely get the words out. In the backyard someone laughed. A girl's voice trilled, "Don't you *dare!*" Someone turned up the music, and it seemed to fill not just the night but the whole world. Standing there on the sidewalk, Eunice felt as if she'd been excluded not only from the party but from the rest of her life. Lumpish, dull, thick-tongued and pierogi-shaped, she was doomed to stand out here forever.

"We—we don't have to go back there." Reggie whispered too. There was another bellow of a laugh, and she shuddered so hard

115

one barrette slipped down over her ear. "We'll just ring the bell, give the cake to his mother, get paid, and get out."

"Right."

"No one will even see us."

"Right."

"We won't have to talk to any of them."

"Right."

But no one answered the bell. Eunice rang it several times, and then Reggie leaned on it for a good thirty seconds; but there was no response.

"She must be out back and can't hear us."

"Now what?"

They both knew, yet they stood on the front steps, frozen, hoping for a tornado to blow the whole party away.

"We're going to have to go around."

"I'll go by myself," said Reggie.

"You can't. You'll panic. You'll puke."

"That's right, I probably will." Reggie was in tears. She took a deep breath and squared her scrawny shoulders. "But if you want me to, I'll do it." She held the cake to her concave chest like a shield. Blinking back tears, she scrubbed at her bird beak of a nose with the back of her hand. In the gathering twilight her shoelaces were radiant.

"I can't let you go puking all over a new customer. You stay here, and I'll take it around."

But when she reached for the cake box, Reggie grasped it all the tighter.

"Reggie, give it to me!"

"You're not the only one who wants to prove they don't mean anything. I want to be free of those yucky creeps too! I want to show 'em too!"

She charged off the steps and around the house. Eunice raced after the flapping beacon of her shoelaces.

The backyard was full of kids, and at first no one noticed Reggie and Eunice. They stood on the edge of the yard, looking in. The guests were gathered near the house, on a patio ringed by flickering kerosene lanterns. The girls stood talking together, while the boys stood around the picnic table, wolfing down chips and dip. Three girls were dancing together, and Eunice recognized them as the ones who, so long ago, had laughed at Joy and her in the burger place. As she watched, a boy broke away from the table and touched one of the girls on the elbow. She spun around and, without missing a beat, began to dance with him. Eunice felt her heart knock against her ribs. *So what?* She told herself. *What's so great about dancing with a boy with dip on his chin? A boy with tortilla chip breath?*

Now another boy made his move, and there were two couples dancing. A girl crossed the patio, and there were three. Eunice could feel the ripple going through them all. What would happen next? The music throbbed; the lanterns flared; Eunice knew the answer. Anything. Everything.

"I don't see Joy and Robert Gray," Reggie, her eyes straight ahead, as stiffly motionless as a deer, hissed out of the corner of her mouth. "I don't see them anywhere. Oh, no. Wait a minute."

From a shadowy corner of the yard, beyond the lanterns, came Robert Gray. Beside him walked a girl in a white dress. but it couldn't be Joy. This girl looked nearly as old as Millie, in that dress, with her hair looped up that way. She didn't plié or pirouette. This girl, slow and majestic as a queen in a procession, matched her every step to Robert's.

This girl didn't just have breasts. She had a *figure*.

Not to mention, her hair was green.

But when she stepped onto the patio and into the flare of light, she frowned Joy's frown, as if for two cents she'd knock over the picnic table and scatter every last one of these gobbling, giggling dumbbells to the wind. As Robert went to help his mother, who was dragging another case of pop out of the garage, this girl folded her arms across her chest and stood tapping one foot. A couple of the girls tried to talk to her, and Eunice could see how she bit off her answers. Turning away, they made faces behind her back. Who wouldn't? She was obviously just suffering these fools till Robert came back out.

117

"Look! Someone's spying on us!" One of the girls pointed. Twenty heads swiveled in Reggie and Eunice's direction.

"Who are they? They're not invited!"

The entire party came charging toward them, and Eunice heard Reggie make a petrified, sobbing sound. She thrust the cake into Eunice's arms and jumped behind her.

"Oh, no, look! It's that girl who has a cake business! I heard about her."

"Yeah, my mother got one of her cheesecakes for her bridge club."

The boys and girls ringed around them.

"Hey, I like your T-shirt."

Eunice was so surprised to hear a compliment she nearly dropped the cake. "Th-thank you," she heard herself say.

"She's Joy's friend, isn't she?"

"I had some of the cheesecake."

"Was that the day you were absent on account of ptomaine poisoning?"

"It was okay. You know, it wasn't *great*, but . . ."

A boy in a blue shirt took a step forward. "You mean, you're running this business single-handed?" he asked Eunice.

"I—I have an ass-assistant."

"You mean partner!" Reggie thrust her head over Eunice's shoulder.

"Oh, no. Are you kidding?" It was Woody Woodpecker from the pool. "Not the Spout!"

They all laughed, even the ones who had been nice a moment before.

"But you're really making money?" went on the boy in the blue shirt. Now Eunice recognized him as the boy who, at the pool, had asked her if she liked soccer. "That's really something. I tried all summer to get a job and couldn't. You're really lucky."

"There's no such thing as luck. It's all elbow grease!" cried Reggie, right in Eunice's ear. "Now look out. We have a delivery to make."

"Somebody call the zoo and tell them their hyena escaped."

"How'd you get started?" the boy in the blue shirt asked Eunice.

"None of your business!" yelped Reggie. "Bug off. We have a cake to deliver!"

"I mean it. What is *she* doing here?"

"Delivering a cake, as anyone with the IQ of a food processor could figure out." The Joy look-alike suddenly loomed up among them. "Now why don't you get out of her way before she drops it?"

The group seemed to melt, clearing a path for Eunice. She and Joy—of course, it really was Joy—were eye to eye. Joy was first to speak.

"Would you like me to take that in to Mrs. Gray for you?"

"I can handle it. I've been delivering cakes by myself for a while now."

The anger in Eunice's voice caught them both off guard. Eunice gripped the cake box, which was again trying to leap from her arms. Was it the quivering lamplight, or did Joy's cheek really twitch?

"I know. I know you have. I just thought . . ." Joy's voice was like a pond in spring: icy on top; trembly liquid beneath. "I know this is a business trip. But—but if you'd like to stay and have a Coke or something . . ."

"We can't! We've got to get going!" The squawk from behind her shoulder made Eunice jump so that the cake box bumped against Joy. Woody Woodpecker exploded into giggles. "We don't have time for stupid, boring parties like this!"

Joy looked past Eunice, and it was obvious she was noticing Reggie for the first time. Her eyes went wide. Her mouth made the shape of an egg.

"Not everybody has time to stand around and laugh at stupid jokes and stuff their faces with junk food, you know!" Seeing Joy's confusion, Reggie got bolder yet. Shrieking into Eunice's ear, she went on. "Not everybody cares so much about being a big shot! Some people have more important things to do with their lives!"

Joy's stare swung to Eunice. Her green hair, if it hadn't been so intricately looped and fastened, would probably have stood on end. The group behind her was laughing and whispering loudly.

"Like swim in their very own built-in pool, all alone."

"Or walk around in their designer scarecrow clothes."

Joy ignored them. "You don't mean . . ." She faltered and shook her head, as if she had water in her ears. "No. I don't believe it."

"You better believe it, Miss Know-It-All. I'm Eunice's new partner, and there's nothing you can do about it!"

"Partners with her? I'd rather be partners with a moray eel!" said Woody Woodpecker.

The titters and whispers buzzing in the background merged with the ringing in Eunice's ears. She could feel Reggie panting on her neck. But all she could see was Joy's stricken face.

"Is she, Eu?" asked Joy quietly. "Is she your partner now?"

Everyone stared at her, waiting for her answer. Behind her Reggie had stopped panting, had stopped, it seemed, breathing at all.

"Is she, Eu? Tell me the truth."

"She—"

"Wow, is this the cake? Great!" Robert Gray bounded up beside Joy. "My mom was just wondering what happened to you."

"We—we experienced some—some technical difficulties and—"

"That's okay, no sweat." Robert Gray paused. He had noticed the look on Joy's face. He glanced at Eunice, then back at Joy. He seemed to make a quick decision. "Hey, Eunice, you're gonna stay for the party, aren't you?"

"She can't!" Reggie's voice reached the shrillest possible human pitch. One note higher, and her vocal cords would snap once and for all. "She can't stay!"

Now it was Robert's turn to notice her. He looked at Eunice as if to ask, What's the joke? Then he said to Reggie, "What do you mean, she can't? Are you her mother or something?"

"She can't. She has to go!"

"Hey, listen, no offense, but this is my party. And if Eunice wants to stay, she can stay."

"Yeah," cried Woody Woodpecker, "She can do whatever she wants!"

"Shut up, Larry," said Robert, then turned back to Reggie. "Understand?"

"She can do whatever she wants!" crowed the Woodpecker.

No, I can't.

"Eu . . ?" said Joy.

"I've gotta go."

"Hey," began Robert Gray, but Eunice thrust the cake box into his arms.

"Here."

Eunice never knew how she got out of that yard, or remembered to pick up her bike, or found her way home. But when she wheeled her bike up her driveway, Reggie was right behind her.

"I know you didn't want to leave, Eu."

"I don't want to talk now. I'm going in."

"They would've let you stay. Not me, but you."

"I didn't want to stay."

"Nobody ever did anything like that for me before. I guess you hate me now for sure."

Eunice turned around.

"Don't say that, okay? I didn't do it just for you. Now I'm going in."

Her parents and Russell were watching TV in the living room. When Russell saw her, he jumped up and grabbed her by the arm.

"It's done, Eu-eu! Come on and see!"

"Not now, Russ."

"But it's done! I finished the world! You have to come look at it!" He was pulling her down the hall to his room. "See?"

There on his desk lay two pieces of blue posterboard, each nearly covered by a huge mound of Play-Doh.

"Russ, I can't—"

"Sit down." He pushed her into the desk chair. "Okay, here we go." He cleared his throat. "First, it was like this."

He fitted the two blobs together. Eunice saw he had managed to make them fit so exactly that only the barest crack showed between. "Everything was one nice, neat piece. The continents fitted together easy as pie. You could walk right from South America to Africa anytime you felt like it." He demonstrated with two fingers. "And then right back." More finger walking.

"But then something happened. It didn't happen all at once, but

121

it sure did happen." He deepened his voice to sound like a narrator in a social studies film. "The heat inside the earth made trouble. There was" —he looked up at his *National Geographic* map on the wall and read— " 'subduction, collision, faulting, and accretion.' And . . . KABOOM!"

Making a horrible grinding noise, he began to part the continents. He made them heave; he made them tremble; he made the voices of people crying out in terror.

"Help! Help! What's happening! There goes South America! There goes Africa! It's the end of the world!"

Russell hummed the beginning of Beethoven's Fifth Symphony. *"Da-da-da-daaaaa!"* Then he abruptly stopped the shuddering and shaking. There it lay, the world broken up into its new, jagged self. "But it wasn't the end. Things were just different, that's all. That's the way it goes on earth. Nothing stays the same. The earth's still hot inside, so who knows what will happen next?" He looked at Eunice as if waiting for her answer. "Who knows?"

"Not me," she whispered.

"That's right. Nobody knows. Some scientists say southern California could get stuck onto Alaska. Some say a whole new continent could rise up out of the Pacific Ocean. All we know for sure is: Things will change. *Ta-daa!* The end!" He dropped his social studies voice and spoke in his normal little-boy one, "Pretty good, huh?" He was so pleased with himself he barely noticed she was already leaving the room. Running a hand over his Play-Doh world, he asked, "Do you think things will ever get back together again, the way they were at first?"

But Eunice was already halfway up the stairs. She didn't want Russell, happy as he was, to see her cry.

Twenty-two

THE NEXT MORNING Eunice lay in bed long after her parents and Millie had left for work. She lay there thinking she might, after all, stay in bed for the rest of her life. If only she could think up an excuse that would convince her parents she should never again have to leave the house. Could she fake leprosy symptoms? Then the phone rang, and Russell called her.

He stood at the bottom of the stairs, holding out the receiver to her. His uncombed hair stood up in spikes, his eyes were still swollen with sleep, and he held a new *National Geographic* to his chest. From the phone at the end of his arm came squealy, staticky sounds like a radio gone haywire.

"It's Reggie," he said. "I think something's wrong."

Eunice took the phone and walked into the kitchen. There on the table was her mother's note, beginning "Good morning! Make sure you and your brother eat a good breakfast." There by her father's place was the newspaper opened to the sports page and the news the Indians were back in the cellar. By Millie's empty teacup was a back-to-school ad for skirts and sweaters. The static was increasing in the receiver. With a heavy sigh Eunice held it to her ear.

"Hello?"

"Guess who just called. You'll never guess. You're not gonna believe this!"

Out of the corner of her eye, through the side door, Eunice thought she saw something move. That was strange. It was too early for the mail. And the something had been too big for one of Russell's friends.

123

"You're not gonna believe it!"

"Believe what?" Eunice craned her neck, trying to see through the starched ruffled curtain on the door.

The something darted. Pulling the phone cord so far she nearly pulled it out of the wall, just as her father always predicted, Eunice caught a glimpse of pale green hair fanning out in the sunshine.

"The board of health, that's who! They want to close us down!"

Eunice dropped the receiver and threw open the screen door. An envelope fluttered to her feet. She ran out to the sidewalk, but the street was deserted. Picking up the envelope, she walked slowly back inside.

"Eu? Did you faint? Are you okay? I told you you wouldn't believe it! Somebody ratted on us! They got a complaint about us operating without a license, and they're sending out an inspector this afternoon!"

Eunice groped her way to a chair and sat down.

"What are we gonna do, Eu? I called my mother, and she said we probably don't have a chance, even if we show them our hairnets and everything."

Eunice opened the envelope. Inside was a crisp ten-dollar bill.

"Who could've double-crossed us like that? All our customers have always been so happy and satisfied! Who could it be? If I ever find out, I'll skin him alive and feed him piece by piece to wild dogs. I'll grind him to crumbs and feed him to the pigeons. I'll—"

"When's the inspector coming?"

"One o'clock. Get over here as fast as you can. I'll start scrubbing everything."

As soon as the inspector strode in the door, clipboard in hand, they knew it was all over. She took one look in the refrigerator and shook her head sternly.

"This is where you're storing your ingredients?" She poked a finger at half an oozy tomato sandwich, leaking onto a paper plate. Beside it stood a dish of mold-covered mushrooms still left from Reggie's birthday party. "And this is your dishwasher? I assume you run bleach through the rinse cycle? Where's the solution you soak your processor in? May I see your medical records? When were your last tine tests?"

"Would you like a nice glass of Hawaiian Punch?"

The inspector, tire-iron straight in her chair, wrote up her report. Eunice, Reggie, and Russell, whom Eunice had had to drag along, watched helplessly.

"Can I ask you one thing?" said Reggie. "Who turned us in?"

"I believe it was an anonymous call."

She handed them a list of twenty-two citations, which they had thirty days to correct. Or else. As soon as she was out the door, Reggie blew up.

"If only I knew who ratted on us! I'd make her eat dirt! I'd break both her legs with a crowbar! I'd . . ."

Eunice saw that any moment now Reggie would burst into tears. "We have to think of it as a compliment, Reg. We were doing so well, we were so professional, the board of health had to take us seriously. She treated us like grown-ups."

Reggie took a swipe at her nose with the hem of her T-shirt.

"Besides, how could we have kept it up? Really, if you think about it. We couldn't ride our bikes in blizzards. How would we deliver stuff?"

"I'd have thought of something."

Eunice sat down beside her. "That's right, you probably would. Knowing you."

Now Reggie leaned forward, her hands clasped between her knees. "Ice cream cakes. We could've made ice cream cakes, and then we could've taken the bus. They wouldn't have melted that fast in winter."

"Okay, but what about school? You know we weren't really going to drop out."

"It would've been complicated. Maybe we would've had to close down—but just temporarily." The tears stood in her pink-lidded eyes. "This—this is permanent, isn't it?"

Eunice knew what she meant. She forced herself to look into Reggie's eyes. "You heard what I said last night. We're partners."

A tear trickled down Reggie's sandpapery cheek. "Oh yeah?"

"Yeah."

Russell, who had been listening closely, began to beam. "That's settled. Let's all go swimming now."

Eunice stood up. "You two go in. I have something to do. I'll be back, though, as soon as I'm done."

"Promise?"

"Make sure you both stay in the shallow end, you hear?"

At the McKenzies' Eunice sat down on the front lawn and waited. Before very long Joy, in her bathing suit and cover-up, came wheeling her bike down the driveway. When she saw Eunice, she stopped and tilted her chin in the air.

"If you're looking for the payment for your cake, Mrs. Gray said she'll mail it to you."

"That's not what I'm here for."

"You're using margarine instead of butter now, aren't you?"

"Yes."

"I could tell."

"No one else can. No one ever complained. We've always had very satisfied customers."

Joy's chin lifted a little higher. "I bet margarine was Reggie's idea."

"That's right."

"Figures."

"A hundred percent satisfied customers. I know what you did, Joy."

"I don't know what you're talking a—"

"You owe Reggie and me a big apology."

"Reggie! I owe Reggie an apology! She's the one who took my place! That whole business was my idea! You were my partner, remember?"

"Things have changed."

"They sure have! You dropped me for her? I can't believe it."

"I never dropped you! You dropped me for Robert!"

"I did not! I told you all along I wanted to stay friends. But you wouldn't. You had to have things just the same as always or not at all. So look what you turn around and do. Take up with her! How

126

do you think that makes me feel, knowing you'd rather be friends with a reject than with me?"

"How do you think it made me feel, seeing you go around with a peanut butter head instead of me?"

"Peanut butter head! What are you talking about?"

"Robert's not your type! He says 'no sweat'! He eats barbecued chips! He made your hair turn green!"

"The pool chlorine did that. If your hair was blond, it'd be just the same. I know you've been spending every day at that reject's!"

"Don't talk about her like that!"

"Why not? It's how you talk about Robert, and you don't even know him."

"I know him as well as you know Reggie!"

At this Joy paused. "That's probably true," she said. Slowly, with pointed toes, she lowered the kickstand on her bike, then sat down beside Eunice on the grass. Pulling her cover-up close around her, she said, "I know Robert seems like a jerk to you. But underneath, he's very sensitive—don't grind your teeth! He really is, for a boy. Last night, when he asked you to stay at the party, he meant it. He could see . . . he could tell . . . he knew I wanted you to." She clutched her cover-up closer yet and went on. "We talk about things when we're alone. He says he can talk to me about things he could never talk to anyone about before."

Eunice felt her throat grow tight with jealousy. "Like what?"

"Like how his mother worries about money so much it drives him crazy and how before every soccer game he gets so scared he almost throws up." She paused, then went on. "And how he remembers being five years old and waking up at dawn, before anyone else. He used to stick his feet out from under the covers and make them talk to each other. One was Mrs. Left and one was Mrs. Right."

"Robert Gray told you that?"

Joy began to pull up grass. "That's when I really like him. But then, when we're with his friends, he's different. He goes along with them. I've spent most of the summer with them, and I still feel like an outsider."

"You do?"

"Yes. And I hate it."

"Now you know a little bit how Reggie feels."

Joy stopped pulling up grass. After a moment she said, "If that's how she feels all the time, no wonder she's such a mess." She scooped the blades of pulled-up grass into a neat little pile. "You mean, you really do like her?"

"It's like you're saying about Robert. There's a part of her nobody guesses is there. And—and . . . I don't know. I think she's changed a little bit. And maybe I have too."

Joy looked up. "I left the party right after you."

"You did?"

"I looked around at those peanut butter heads, and I missed you so much I thought I'd expire on the spot."

"I missed you, too, Joy. Boy, did I."

They looked at each other, across years of friendship.

"I'm sorry for what I did. As soon as I called the health department, I couldn't believe I'd done such a scummy thing. I tried to call them back and tell them it was probably a crank call, but they didn't seem to believe me. Then I went over your house to apologize. And to try to pay you back. But I got too scared. I remembered how you stood up to all those kids last night, and I was afraid to face you. Do you think the health department will come and check?"

"They already did. Have Your Cake's kaput."

"Oh no. They don't waste any time, do they? I bet you made a lot of money, though, didn't you?"

"I don't even know how much we've made. We've just been dividing it every time, not adding it up."

"What are you going to do with your share?"

Eunice realized she'd never thought about that. "I don't know. I guess if I was a real entrepreneur, I'd reinvest it, right? Start another business?"

"With her?"

Eunice scooped up the little pile of grass Joy had made. "Maybe. If she wanted." She paused. "But I don't think there's any law against having a three-way partnership."

"I am going to need some money. I've been thinking. I might want those private lessons after all."

Eunice jumped to her feet and pulled Joy up beside her. "Come on. Reggie's waiting for me. We can brainstorm. We'll have an executive board meeting. She and I have the capital to start something *really* big this time."

Joy took a step back. "Listen, Eu, that sounds interesting, but . . . I have a better idea. Remember that boy at the party last night, the one in the blue shirt with the crinkly hair? His name is Joe. After you left, he asked me if I could get you to come to the pool today."

"What for?"

"What do you think, goofy? He pretended it was because he wanted to ask you more questions about starting your own business, but I know it's because he likes you."

"Likes me? Me?"

"Eunice Enid Gottlieb, egad! Is that so astonishing?"

"You must have bribed him. Or blackmailed him."

"You can't bribe or blackmail somebody into liking you. Joe's very acceptable. He wants to be a vet. Robert probably likes him the best of all the guys. I thought we could all meet and then go get ice cream together. What do you think?"

I think this is the pure, exact opposite of how the Unvarnished Truth is supposed to work. Life is being kind. People are caring. Friendship is lurking where I least expected it. Look out.

"Well? I'm supposed to be there right now. We could whiz past your house, get your suit, and—"

And leave Reggie hanging on the edge of the pool, panting and waiting. She'd wait until dark. She'd wait all night and all tomorrow. That's how loyal she is.

"I can't, Joy."
"Why not?"

"I promised her."

"And I promised Robert."

They looked at each other again, across all those years of friendship, all those pages in the red and white scrapbook.

"Did you promise Reggie for tomorrow too?"

"No."

"Then maybe you could come to the pool tomorrow."

"And maybe the next day you could come to Reggie's."

"Well," said Joy, "we'll see."

And then she suddenly reached out and gave Eunice one of her old, familiar bone-crushing hugs. Tears popped into Eunice's eyes.

Joy rode Eunice on her bike to the corner where they had to go in separate directions.

"Au reservoir!"

"Au reservoir!"

And they parted.

Twenty-three

WHEN EUNICE WALKED into the Ackeroyds' backyard, Reggie was standing on the edge of the diving board. Even from across the lawn Eunice could see her knees knocking and her teeth chattering.

"Reggie! I'm here! I'm back! What are you doing?"

Reggie turned toward her and gave a very weak wave. She took a small bounce on the board and nearly lost her balance.

"Reggie, stop! Get off there! You'll kill yourself!"

But it was too late. Reggie, a flaming orange kamikaze, was already in the air. Eunice, frozen with horror, saw a dozen scenes of Reggie's demise flash before her: Reggie cracking her chin on the board, Reggie grinding her skull against the bottom of the pool. . . .

Reggie slipped into the water like a sharp little knife.

"Hurray!" cheered Russell, who was sitting on the edge of the shallow end. "Just like on *Wide World of Sports!*"

Reggie surfaced and thrashed her way to the side. When Eunice ran to her she looked up, red-eyed and grinning.

"Hi!" she said, trying and completely failing to sound casual. "What's new?"

"She's been practicing the whole time you were gone," said Russell, coming up beside her. "I told her she was supposed to stay in the shallow end, but she wouldn't listen. She said, 'Russ-o, you can't be a whining wimp if you expect to get anywhere in the world.' " He looked at Reggie with shining eyes.

"You mean you learned to dive like that this afternoon?" asked Eunice.

"Are you crazy?" cried Reggie. She hoisted herself out of the pool and wrapped herself in her big orange towel. "I've been practicing almost since that first day you and Joy came here." She burped. "Yuck. I swallowed half the pool today."

"I didn't know you were practicing."

"First I started doing it because you made me so mad. I figured if I could learn to dive, I'd show you I wasn't a complete nothing." She burped again. "But now . . ." She shrugged, then suddenly dropped her towel and ran back to the board. Without any hesitation at all this time she walked to the end, bounced once, and sliced neatly through the water.

This time when she surfaced, Eunice reached a hand to help her out, knowing she must be exhausted. But Reggie shook her head.

"I want to practice my strokes a little bit," she said through lips the color of prune plums. "You never know when you might fall out of a boat or something."

Eunice went inside and changed into Lydia's jade green suit. And then the water world let her in too.

Twenty-four

THE ENVELOPE WAS there, on the kitchen table, addressed in her own carefully disguised handwriting. Eunice snatched it up, ran to the bathroom, and locked the door.

DEAR REJECT II:
  People very rarely stay best friends with the same person all their lives. Though your friend has hurt you, remember this: God never closes a door without opening a window.

Eunice leaned against the locked bathroom door and read the reply over and over again. Two sentences, that was all. Even knowing that this paper must have been in Dear Phoebe's very hands didn't help. What a gyp! Phoebe had used that line about opening a window countless times before. She might as well have sent Eunice a form letter.

Eunice tore the letter into tiny pieces and flushed them down the toilet. Then she sat on the edge of the bathtub and stared at her crooked big toe. The letter was a gyp, all right, and she was furious.

She sat there a long while, and slowly the fury turned to anger. Then the anger turned to irritation. The longer she thought about it, the harder it became to blame Dear Phoebe. How did the woman keep on doing her job anyway? Day after day, year after year, trying to solve other people's problems—it wasn't human. It was a superhero's task. Who could blame her if she got tired? If she ran out of clever remarks? Who could be surprised if after all this time she saw similarities in people's troubles and gave out one-size-fits-all advice?

Eunice looked down at her inherited big toe. She thought of Reggie, Joy, even Robert Gray, who had troubles he'd never told anyone before Joy. Each of them knew how it felt to be an outsider. To feel all alone. They all had to find, when they came up against that closed door, the open window. Maybe that was why her anger against Dear Phoebe was slowly ebbing away. Because her generic reply had some truth in it. Because people *were* alike after all.

Knock knock!

"Eunice? I have to take my shower. *Now!*"

Eunice stood up and slowly did a few we-must-improve-our-bust exercises. Millie pounded again.

"Eunice, open this door this minute or I'll tell Mom who broke her Mixmaster."

Eunice opened the door and Millie, armed with all the ammunition she needed to get ready for a date, sailed by her. Eunice thought of tomorrow, when she was supposed to go to the pool with Joy to meet Joe. Should she curl her eyelashes too? With her luck she'd probably break them all off. She could pray she wouldn't get lockjaw the minute he said hi.

From down the hall came a grinding and muttering, and she saw Russell, hunched over his desk, breaking the world in half.

"And who knows?" he was asking his invisible audience. "Who knows where the shifting plates will take us next?"

Eunice went out and sat on the front steps. Who knew? was right. There was a cidery tang in the air tonight, and Dear Phoebe's column had been surrounded by back-to-school ads. Tomorrow she was going to the pool with Joy. The next day she and Reggie would discuss their new business. For now she could keep the two worlds separate, but what was going to happen in two weeks, when school started? Who knew? was right.

Russell, still mumbling to himself, came out and sat beside her. He was eating one of his frozen peanut butter and marshmallow creations, and he gave her a bite. It was good. It made her teeth hurt, but it was good. Eunice took another bite, and though the evening was growing cool and the frozen peanut butter made her shiver, a small warmth grew inside her. Somehow things would work out. Somehow she'd find a way to "This above all: to her own self be true." Was that why Dear Phoebe's letter didn't irk her more? Because, somehow, she didn't need Phoebe quite as much as she used to? Because, somehow, she was starting to figure a few things out for herself?

She took another bite, and a little chill went down her spine. Of course, she wouldn't feel like this tomorrow. Tomorrow she'd be in a cold sweat, thinking about school starting. That was the way life went. Not one feeling or thought was guaranteed to last. That was what made a person's head spin. That was what made life so confusing. It wasn't, she'd tell Russell someday, just the continents. All of life trembled, heaved, shuddered and slipped, so that no one could tell from one day to the next where it would separate, and where connect.

But changes weren't the end of the world. She took another shivery bite. Sometimes changes could be only the beginning.

And that, thought Eunice, was the truth.

ABOUT THE AUTHOR

TRICIA SPRINGSTUBB is the author of numerous short stories, picture books, and young adult novels, including *Give and Take* and *The Moon on a String*. Several years ago, when she was a writer-in-residence at a local elementary school, she created the characters Eunice and Joy, two irrepressible and imaginative best friends. Their adventures will appear as a trilogy. *Eunice Gottlieb and the Unwhitewashed Truth about Life* follows *Which Way to the Nearest Wilderness?*, the first book about Eunice and Joy.

Ms. Springstubb lives in Cleveland Heights, Ohio, with her husband and three children, Zoe, Phoebe, and Delia.